CW00584637

TEEN DREAMS
AND WHAT THEY MEAN

anna jaskolka

quantum

An imprint of W. Foulsham & Co. Ltd
The Publishing House, Bennetts Close, Cippenham,
Slough, Berkshire, SL1 5AP, England

ISBN 0-572-02877-6

Copyright © 2003 Anna Jaskolka

The moral right of the author has been asserted.

All rights reserved.

The Copyright Act prohibits (subject to certain very limited exceptions) the making of copies of any copyright work or of a substantial part of such a work, including the making of copies by photocopying or similar process. Written permission to make a copy or copies must therefore normally be obtained from the publisher in advance. It is advisable also to consult the publisher if in any doubt as to the legality of any copying which is to be undertaken.

You can photocopy the worksheet on pages 160–1 for your personal use only.

Printed in Great Britain by St Edmundsbury Press, Bury St Edmunds, Suffolk

Contents

Introduction

Dreams are magical and mysterious and a constant source of wonder. No matter where in the world we are or what we are doing, every night when we go to bed and fall asleep, we enter another world: the magical world of dreams.

As you know only too well, life isn't always easy when you're a teenager. In today's world there are constant changes to keep up to date with, and you are bombarded with new information to absorb, not least at school, where there is that vital coursework to complete and life-changing exams to sit. Your life is busy with friends, work, football, fashion, television, computers, mobile phones, future plans and aspirations – the list is endless. Add to this the fact that the teenage years are an emotionally changeable time and can feel traumatic. Not only are you dealing with the physical aspects of growing up, with all those fluctuating hormones, but you are also dealing with the emotional transition from childhood into adulthood.

With all this physical and emotional activity going on in your waking life, it's not surprising that your dreams are likely to be especially vivid and memorable. And it might also be true to say that younger people are often more in tune with the magic and mysterious nature of the inner dream world.

It was when I was working in live television with younger viewers that it became apparent to me how fascinated most teenagers are by their dreams. The young people I talked to on the *CBBC Xchange* programme were keen to know what their dreams meant and how they could use them to help to make sense of their everyday lives. We were amazed at the overwhelming number of teenagers who contacted us for help in explaining their dreams. We looked for books about dreams specifically for young people – and found nothing. Despite the fact that there are many books published on dreams, none seemed to be focused on the fast, modern lifestyle of the young.

So that's how I came to be writing this book, which is designed specifically for teenagers and young people, to help you understand why you dream, what your dreams are trying to tell you, and how to interpret those messages and put them into practice to improve your everyday life.

I had this really strange dream ...

Of course, we take dreaming for granted because we dream every night of our lives, even though some of us might never remember dreaming at all. Some of us dream in colour, some in black and white. Some dreams are realistic, some surreal and some are even cartoons! All our dreams are totally unique, and we are the only person in the audience of our very own picture show.

I believe that one of the functions of dreaming is to clear the clutter from our minds, emptying them of all the thoughts and feelings of the day, so even though we may not remember the dreams, we have still benefited from them. The other, major function of dreams is to transmit messages from our subconscious to our conscious mind. Dreams are our deepest intuitions trying to communicate with us.

Occasionally a dream will catch our attention because it is odd, vivid or even disturbing, and we may dwell on it for some time. It may even stay with us for many days. We will probably feel the urge to tell someone about it, in the hope that they can help us make sense of it. The dream may come back more than once, making us all the more determined to find out its meaning, or we may experience several different dreams, all with what appears to be a similar message.

I believe that such dreams are there to help us; they are messages from our subconscious that can enable us to understand more about ourselves and to look honestly at how we are feeling. A dream may be highlighting feelings that we have been hiding but which would be better brought out into the open. It may be showing us what we need to do to cope with a difficult situation. It may be reminding us that it's OK to be nervous or unsure of ourselves, or it may be telling us that something really exciting is about to happen. If the message is important enough, your subconscious will try all kinds of routes until it eventually gets through.

How frustrating it is when you can't grasp what that crucial meaning is! My intention in writing this book is to help you work out what your dreams are trying to tell you. Only the dreamer can interpret what any dream really means for them, but after several years of listening to people explain their dreams to me, I have worked out a simple method that you can use to help you understand the language of your dreams.

the language of dreams

Our ultra-funky modern lifestyles no longer seem to allow us time just to chill out and count the clouds. How often do we notice the colour of the sky or the smell of newly cut grass? We are more likely to be caught up in listening to the latest single, finding out the football results or discussing who has the trendiest mobile phone and just how much we want one too! But the language of dreams hasn't changed throughout our time on earth; it still talks to us through ancient symbolism. In order to understand what a dream is trying to tell us, we need to switch our brains into dream language.

In dream language we rarely use words; it's like playing charades – we communicate through actions and images. Let me give you an example. Let's say, for instance, that you have been meaning to ring a girlfriend but you have been putting it off for far too long – and let's say a bit of guilt has crept in. So how is your subconscious mind going to get you to make the phone call? Well, how do we get in touch with people? Mostly by telephone, so – switching into dream language – in your dream you will have a mobile phone. It's important that you call this person, so we will make it a really funky, all-singing, all-dancing mobile that features as the star of the dream, and we will make it mega big. Who is it you're calling? A girlfriend, so let's make it a bright pink mobile. Your subconscious wants to tell you that when you eventually make the call, it's going to be great fun, so let's make the ring tone a hit by someone you really love, like Kylie Minogue. What about the tune of 'I just can't get you out of my head'?

Get the idea? When you want to interpret a dream, you need to work it out in dream language – and that's what I'll be explaining in this book.

dream themes

We will also be looking at some universal themes that crop up frequently in our dreams, such as fire, water, wind, colours and so on. These are images that have a common meaning for all of us, no matter where we live and how old we are. During my exciting time dealing live on TV with your dreams, I have collected an extensive range of examples, some of which we will be looking at later.

the magic of dreaming

Throughout history, dreams have been used as divine inspiration. Seers have used dreams to forecast feasts and famine, war and peace. Many considered dreams to be messages from the gods. Artists and creative people of all kinds have used dreams to help them paint, write and draw. The Beatles were inspired by their dreams, and how many artists have said 'It came to me in a dream'? *Alice in Wonderland* is one of my favourite books, as when reading it I always feel as though I am walking in someone else's dream! I'll be looking at these magical aspects of dreaming too.

nightmares

Young people seem to have more nightmares than older people do, so they are especially important for you to understand. Considering the immense amount of change going on in your life, it isn't surprising that the stresses and strains come out in the form of nightmares, which can be extremely frightening. Some people claim that nightmares have no significance and even put them down to indigestion. I don't dismiss them in this way, but neither do I believe they're anything to be alarmed about. If you want to catch someone's attention and they're not listening, what do you do? Shout at them, wave your arms in the air, do something outrageous perhaps? I believe nightmares are just your subconscious doing the same. More about this later.

how to use this book

We often suppress our feelings, so that most people would never guess that the clever, confident person they see and know so well is really terrified of talking to a teacher about a disappointing exam result, making a phone call about a weekend job or leaving home and going off to university. Your friends may see you as dynamic and successful while you are having dreams that show a very different side to your nature.

So what is the point of trying to understand these dreams? Firstly, understanding yourself and admitting to what you truly think and feel is a really important part of growing up. It's desirable to be clever and confident, but it's also healthy to admit that there are things that make you quake in your boots and to learn how to deal with them – all of your feelings are part of the complex and wonderful person you are. Secondly, if you know that you are nervous, then you can learn to give yourself a little extra tender loving care, or you may feel able to share your concerns with someone – your mum or your best friend perhaps. After all, the message in your dream could be a reminder to ask for help and support when you need it – and we all do sometimes.

In this book, we'll be taking a fresh, up-to-date approach to your dreams. We'll be using the knowledge that has been acquired throughout the ages in order to bring the fascinating world of dreaming into our fast modern life. To do this, we'll be making use of a method that I have worked out to take you right to the heart of your dream and, with any luck, help you to discover its message.

It's sad when we lose touch with our inner magic. If you feel that you've lost touch with yours, I hope to be able to reconnect you, as well as to reassure you that dreams, for all their strangeness and mystery, are truly there to help, guide and inspire you.

What Happens When We Fall Asleep?

In this chapter we're going to take a look at the mechanics of sleep – what actually happens to our bodies as we doze off.

We all know that we need to sleep; common sense tells us that. Yet though much research has been done in this field, it is still not known why we fall asleep each night. There are many theories, such as the need for rest, regeneration and growth, but no one is absolutely certain of the truth. What we do know is that during sleep the metabolic rate and blood pressure drop, and a considerable amount of hormonal activity occurs. This is responsible for tissue repair and growth.

Why do we feel tired? Why are we unable to stay awake indefinitely? This question has remained almost a complete mystery for centuries, even to modern scientists. However, scientists have now made a significant discovery in the shape of a molecule called orexin, which is produced in the brain. This molecule controls sleepiness. After a good night's sleep when the body is rested, this molecule is released quickly and in large quantities throughout our brain; it literally tells the brain to wake up. During the day, the molecule slowly disappears from the brain, and when it runs out, the brain starts to shut down and we feel tired. Drugs will eventually be developed by scientists that mimic orexin. These could have many applications: such as curing people of sleep disorders and keeping pilots alert during long flights. The discovery of this drug also opens up the possibility to being able to stay awake for long periods, although whether that would have other ill-effects, we don't know. In any event, who would want to miss out on their dreams for so long?

do we need sleep?

There are a number of centres throughout the world whose main objective is to study the sleeping and dreaming process. Here, people with dream and sleep problems are monitored and the resulting information is analysed. In addition, students who need to earn a bit of extra cash are often invited to act as guinea pigs in research into dreams and sleep behaviour.

Studies have been undertaken in which these human guinea pigs are kept awake for several days at a time to see what happens to them without sleep. It is reported that without sleep a person can still function, but their memory starts to falter, their speech starts to slur and they suffer from dizziness and slow co-ordination. They will also suffer from mood swings and irritability. It's better to get a good night's sleep!

The longest time a person has been officially deprived of sleep is 11 days. When eventually allowed to drift off to sleep, this person suffered no ill effects and in time managed to catch up on their sleep. Nevertheless, if you are studying for exams it's far better to take an early night and benefit from a clear-thinking head in the morning rather than trying to stay awake in order to cram in lots of revision. A night of quality sleep enables you to perform at optimum levels the following day.

The amount of sleep we need varies from person to person. Margaret Thatcher, a former prime minister of Great Britain, was reported only to sleep for four hours each night and still perform all her duties with gusto. Similarly, another former British leader, Winston Churchill, reportedly survived and flourished on very little sleep. However, we lesser mortals will probably find that we need far more sleep than that. And regardless of how little sleep we need as individuals, no living creature can go without sleep indefinitely.

We tend to need less sleep as we grow older. Babies and small children – just like small animals of all kinds such as puppies and kittens – spend huge amounts of time sleeping, waking up mainly in order to feed. This is thought to be simply because they need to direct all their energy into growth. By the time we reach adulthood we will probably require between five and nine hours sleep each night.

As we move into old age, the need for night-time sleep in particular tends to decrease. My mother, who is in her seventies, is a great example of this. She gets up each day at the crack of dawn, around 5am. She does all her housework and is ready for a snooze at around 9.30am, when the rest of the household has just got up! She has several naps during the day and sleeps very little at night. Of course, everyone has their own unique sleep pattern, but it does appear that older people need less sleep overall.

the pattern of sleep

Some of the research that is being done on sleep is conducted by the use of EEG (electroencephalograph). This is an instrument used to monitor the electrical activity of the brain. It has wires, which are attached to the sleeping person's head, and these record the electrical activity occurring in the brain during the sleep cycle. Through working with EEG, scientists have discovered that there are four distinct stages of sleep:

- ◎ **Stage one sleep:** the stage between being awake and being asleep. Brain patterns have slowed down to alpha waves. (This is the pattern of brain activity found in states of hypnosis.)

- ◎ **Stage two sleep:** this is normal sleep. Brain patterns have slowed down further still; there are tiny regular bursts of activity.

- ◎ **Stage three sleep:** NREM – non rapid eye movement. At this stage it would be very difficult to wake the sleeper as they are in a very deep sleep.

- ◎ **Stage four sleep:** REM – rapid eye movement. This is the dreaming state.

During a night's sleep we go through the above cycle several times, spending about six hours in NREM and two hours in REM sleep during a typical eight-hour sleeping cycle. We can deduce from this that most of us will dream about 10 times each night.

When people say they never dream, the truth is that they just don't remember their dreams. This is because they don't wake up during REM sleep (they may be waking during other stages of sleep). Experiments have shown that if 'non-dreamers' are woken up during their REM cycle they are able to recall vivid dreams.

During sleep your brain is still active and working (as is shown by EEG experiments), and your body is still carrying out many functions. The digestive system goes on processing food, and (except during REM sleep; more on this on page 17) the muscles continue to work – you can toss and turn in your sleep. Your reflexes continue working; for example if you have an itch when you are asleep, you will still scratch it. Your hearing is still functioning – if there is a loud noise or a telephone rings you will wake up.

the quality of sleep

You will know from experience that after a few restless nights and periods of sleeplessness, you will feel much better for a good night's sleep. It has always been thought we need to sleep in order to rest the body and the mind. This is indeed the case to a certain degree; however, as we've already noted, the body still functions and the mind is still quite active throughout the duration of sleep. Maybe we need to sleep in order to dream.

restful sleep

It is thought that it is during the NREM cycle (stage three) that we receive the bulk of our rest and recuperation. In tests, people who have been deprived of NREM sleep become clumsy and awkward and their physical co-ordination deteriorates. Interestingly, those who have been deprived of REM sleep seem to suffer adverse effects on a mental level, experiencing confusion, inability to concentrate and loss of memory.

But if getting too little sleep can be detrimental, sleeping for too long can also have an adverse effect on you. As we've already noted, an adult needs on average between five and nine hours sleep per night. Getting more sleep than that can leave you feeling de-energised, lethargic and mentally dull. So when you're tempted to lie in and snooze under the duvet, remember that too much sleep is not good for you!

disrupted sleep

What a complicated, complex and intriguing species we humans are! You would think after everything we've discussed so far that if you manage to get your ration of, say, eight hours sleep you will be fine, but it's not as simple as that. Ask anyone who works during the night or who works on a shift rota. Try asking parents who have to get up several times every night to feed and attend to the needs of babies or young children.

People who work during the night often find it impossible to sleep during the day, and – like people who have their sleep interrupted frequently – suffer from a variety of side-effects, such as weight loss, bad temper, lack of concentration, skin complaints and nervousness. Attempting to catch up on a few hours sleep during the day can never quite make up for a solid eight hours sleep at night.

The body works to its own rhythm and has its own internal body clock, which is linked externally to the earth's orbit. Your body expects a routine – regular periods of activity during daylight followed by sleep at night. When that rhythm is broken, your body clock goes 'out of sync' and this causes sleep disturbance. We suffer jet lag for precisely this reason: when we cross time zones, the rhythm of day and night is broken; the body cannot adjust immediately and we become temporarily 'out of sync', feeling tired, irritable and generally out of sorts. Once back in a regular pattern, the body quickly recovers and normal sleep resumes.

Working long hours, staying awake at night and trying to sleep in the day cause lots of adverse side-effects. While none of these is major, we don't need laboratory reports on scientific trials to tell us that a good night's sleep is far better than a good day's sleep. The human body is intricately programmed to sleep regularly at night.

rapid eye movement (REM)

Have you ever been watching someone sleeping when all at once their eyes start to move under their eyelids? It's as though they're watching something even though their eyelids are closed. The movements can be very fast indeed. This is a sure sign that they are dreaming. If you woke them up at this sleep stage they would be able to recall their dream quite vividly, although they might not be too happy about being woken up!

I often watch my dog sleeping by the fire and I can tell right away when she is dreaming. Her eyes will be moving quickly beneath her eyelids and her legs give little twitches.

I have the feeling she's dreaming about chasing rabbits across the fields.

To prepare for REM sleep the body adjusts its patterns of physical and mental activity. The blood flow to the brain increases, as does the temperature of the brain itself. Breathing and heartbeat become irregular. During REM sleep, the sexual organs of both males and females are stimulated. Another important change is that the body is paralysed. This is thought to be a safety mechanism – if, for example, you are dreaming about flying, this deactivation prevents you from physically trying to do so. (It follows, therefore, that a person who is sleepwalking cannot possibly be dreaming at that time.) It does occasionally happen that on waking from a period of REM sleep the body is immobilised. This phenomenon is understandably worrying if it happens to you; however, there is actually no need to be concerned; the sensation lasts for only a fleeting moment before normal feeling returns. Recent studies of subjects who say they have been abducted by aliens have put down their experiences to hallucinating whilst in this stage of sleep paralysis.

dreaming

Dreaming has always been part of our lives. When humans first appeared on this planet, falling asleep when the sun went down and waking up when the sun rose was (and still is) the most natural thing to do. Dreaming was an accepted part of that natural cycle. Archaeologists have found dream artwork from as early as the stone age, and we have written evidence of dreams and dream meanings dating back to 668 BCE in Assyria. We have been fascinated by the magic of dreams from the beginning of time.

In modern times, our knowledge has developed to such a degree that we can use medical and scientific techniques to look into what happens to our bodies and brains when we go to bed at night. We now know the mechanics of sleep; however, our dream world remains a bottomless well of fascinating mystery.

Each night you drift off into a state of unconsciousness. During this time your brain and body operate without your conscious knowledge, carrying you off into nightly adventures in which you experience your own unique dream world until slowly but surely you wake up each morning.

The History of Dreams

Ever since time began, dreams have been a magical source of mystery and wonder. Many ancient civilisations are known to have placed great importance on dreams and made great efforts to interpret and understand them. Originally dreams were thought to be prophetic messages sent from the gods. Dreamers were encouraged to share their dreams, as it was thought that they could hold important messages for the whole nation, forewarning people of events, both good and bad, that were yet to unfold. Dream temples and places of worship were built in order to house prophets and wise people whose lives were dedicated to the interpretation of dreams.

Fastidious rituals were often performed to evoke dreaming in a person, with the aim of channelling messages from the gods. Days of fasting, meditation and prayer would be part of the rites observed, as the cleansing of both mind and body was thought necessary to communicate with divinities. Great council was held, where people gathered for days to tell one another their dreams and discover their messages and symbolic meanings. Though many dreams were personal in nature, some were thought to hold significant messages for the whole country, and these were reported back to the national leaders.

At around the time of the seventh or eighth Egyptian dynasty, about 2150 BCE, the great famine of Egypt was foreseen in such a dream. This dream involved an image of seven fat and contented cattle, followed by an image of seven cattle that were thin, lean and starving. The interpretation was that the seven fat cows represented seven years of good crops, meaning that food would be plentiful for seven years.

The thin starving cattle warned that seven years of famine and drought would follow. The Pharaoh believed this dream and took immediate action. During the plentiful years, he saw to it that grain was stored and that drainage and irrigation systems were constructed in preparation for the drought. In this instance, the foresight of the Pharaoh saved the population from a potential disaster, for there were indeed seven plentiful years followed by seven years of drought. If the Pharaoh had not heeded the warning in this dream, his people would have suffered seven years of hardship, starvation and death.

Many such great dreams have been recorded in the annals of history. In the 19th century, archaeologists recovered clay tablet scripts from the ancient Assyrian library of Nineveh. Some of these clay scripts, dated 2000 BCE, are thought to represent attempts to record dreams and interpret their meanings. By the time of the 12th dynasty (1937–1759 BCE), the ancient Egyptians had published a book on dream symbols. They had also erected dream temples for their gods to deliver their messages in splendour.

Dreams are common throughout the Bible, where they are also seen as prophetic messages with symbolic importance. Joseph was told in a dream that Mary would bear a child of God and that he was to marry her. Later, he was also warned in a dream to escape from the grasp of Herod, who wanted to kill the baby Jesus. Herod himself was prompted to kill Jesus by a dream, in which he saw the child being made king. Herod was terrified that the child would take over his throne. You will probably be familiar with the story of Herod ordering the execution of all infant male children under the age of two years. Jesus only escaped this terrible fate because Joseph took heed of his own dream and made sure that baby Jesus would not be found.

The course of history has been influenced throughout millennia by people who have heeded the messages hidden within their dreams.

why were dreams so important in ancient times?

Let's go back to a time when we had no technology and try to visualise how different life would be. Let's take a journey back to ancient Egypt.

There are no roads, only sand tracks through the desert. Most of the population live in small huts with their extended family, together with their animals and livestock. Living by the great River Nile is a necessity, as this is the only source of water in the land that can sustain human life and vegetation. Fresh drinking water is scarce and has to be carried from the well in goatskin vessels. There is no sanitation.

The days are long and hot. Working on the land from sunrise to sunset is the normal way of life for most people. To get supplies and exchange goods means going to market; this is a long journey on foot and can take several days. Travellers and traders pass by occasionally, carrying their goods on their heads. If you are wealthy enough, you may have a beast of burden to carry your goods to market. Going to market is exciting, and this is where you catch up on the latest gossip and news.

If you live closer to the great city, you will work for the Pharaoh and the upkeep of the city. Most men and young boys are commandeered by the Pharaoh and placed in his army, leaving their homes for the big city as soon as they are of age. It may be years before the family ever sees them again. They will hopefully return one day and tell their stories of journeys to other lands.

Word of mouth is the only way that you ever find out about anything. News arrives in the form of passing travellers and will probably be months if not years old. Despite the small distance to the sea, most people never witness it in their lifetime. Journeys by sea are only attempted by the Pharaoh's ships. Observing the stars and changes in the heavens is your only method of measuring changes in time and the passing of seasons and years.

If you need to send a message, this will be done by word of mouth; paper is not an item that an ordinary person has access to, and of course most people do not know how to write. You will ask a neighbour or a passing traveller to take the message for you, knowing that it could be weeks or months before your message arrives, if indeed it ever does.

The nightly world of dreams plays a large role in everyone's lives. People live simple lives and are very in tune with nature and the land; they have to be for survival. Their lives revolve around their gods – praying to them, building temples, visiting temples, and performing rituals and sacrifices to honour and appease them. Good weather, plentiful harvests and for the sun to rise each morning are the main subjects of prayers.

As dreams are thought to come directly from the gods, dreaming is of vital importance. People look to their dreams for omens both good and bad, for guidance in their lives and for protection for themselves and their families. Dreaming is an important and often life-saving form of communication. Premonition dreams are bountiful, and many are recorded in the temples.

wisdom of the ancients

There is a tendency for modern-day scientists to dismiss the ideas and thoughts of ancient civilisations. However, our ancestors were no less intelligent or capable than us. They navigated by the stars, had considerable knowledge of the solar system, built structures such as the pyramids, and had mathematical and construction skills as advanced as those we have today.

Their dream world was an important part of their daily lives and was often a helpful tool in their battles for survival and struggle for success. Their knowledge about dreams was gained not in a methodical scientific manner, since the scientific methodology we use today was not developed until modern times, but was slowly and surely gleaned from careful observation and personal experience.

They did not have high-tech meteorological equipment, so frequently their only way of knowing that a great famine was coming was through a premonition dream. They did not have sophisticated electronic news media, so a dream was often their only warning if their land was about to be invaded. They relied on their temple priests and wise seers to inform them of impending doom or triumph, and this was achieved by interpretation of dreams and visions.

the importance of dreams today

In modern culture, technology such as the internet, television and mobile phones has taken away the need for us to pay so much attention to our dream world. We now usually get plenty of electronic warning about what is going to happen. Experts monitor weather patterns and world events constantly, and our televisions and radios can bring us instant coverage of any event in any part of the world. The internet enables us to get information instantly from places on the other side of the world and communicate quickly with people who live there.

These days, governments, politicians, schools and so on oversee our day-to-day survival and safety. Our whole social structure is set up to protect us, and we no longer have to take much notice of our dream world for insight and guidance about matters of national importance and the patterns of the seasons, unless of course we want to.

The world is becoming a faster and faster place. We now routinely experience tremendous technological advances, and yet take them for granted. Nevertheless, there is one notable thing that has seen little change throughout much of our history on this planet, and that is the human body. Human physiology has stayed almost the same for thousands and thousands of years, and those changes that have occurred have been gradual and subtle – such as the appendix becoming smaller. In general, our bodies, organs and brains have barely altered at all, so we can safely assume that we dream in much the same way that our distant ancestors did. The difference is that we no longer tend to attach great significance to dreams; we do not feel the need to scrutinise them and do not depend on them for guidance in our daily fight for survival.

recent history

The growth of Christianity in the Middle Ages had a very detrimental effect on the role of dreams within society. The Christian church proclaimed that dreams were the work of the devil and a product of sorcery. From this period onwards dreaming ceased to be seen as an important part of our culture; dreams were now demonised and placed in a similar category to witchcraft and paganism. Still today our attitude towards dreams is marked by this stigmatisation.

Only within the last 150 years or so has interest in dreams been rekindled and study resumed. The following psychoanalysts have all contributed greatly to our modern understanding of the dream process.

Sigmund Freud (1865–1939)

The interpretation of dreams played a central role in Freud's pioneering psychoanalytic work. According to him, dreams are wish-fulfilling and mirror our deepest desires. He also believed fervently that almost all dreaming is sexual in content. According to Freud, all long pointed objects in our dreams are symbolic of the penis, and all deep hollow objects represent the vagina.

Alfred Adler (1870–1937)

Adler worked alongside Freud for a considerable time and he too was instrumental in forming our modern-day beliefs about dreaming. His view was that each person has unique feelings and that deep down we all want to get the best out of our lives. He felt that dreams could help us to do this. It was Adler who coined the phrase 'inferiority complex'. He believed that by understanding our dreams we could begin to understand our complexes and ourselves.

Carl Gustav Jung (1875–1961)

Jung also worked alongside Freud for several years but disagreed fundamentally with Freud's theory on the sexual content of dreaming. Jung believed that each dream is unique to the dreamer and that only the dreamer can work out its true meaning – by unravelling its symbolism. He regarded dreams as messages from ourselves to ourselves that can teach us about our desires and our longings.

Here, with Jung's view, we have what I believe to be the true nature of dreaming: dreams are messages from ourselves to ourselves. We remember our dreams because we need to learn something from them; there is always a message there waiting to be understood.

So What Exactly Is a Dream?

A dream, as we all know, is a collection of images in the mind's eye that appear to us in our sleep. The images can be seen in isolation but more often they follow some sort of story line.

Unlike waking reality, which is structured and adheres to the physical laws of time and space, the dream world knows no boundaries, and in it anything can and does happen without any logical reason. The sky can be blood red. You can be walking on a road of sunflowers one moment, and the next you can be naked in the kitchen having a cup of hot chocolate with a TV celebrity. The world of dreams can be exciting, adventure filled, informative and sensual, but it can also show a flip side, becoming in an instant a weird and frightening place.

More often than not, you will appear in your own dream, because dreams are about you. It is as though you have been set free within your own virtual-reality cinema and the laws of nature are no more. You can fly through the air; you can zoom off to other worlds in a spilt second; you can be walking in your own future and your own past at the same time.

Once you become familiar with your dream world you can even begin to take control. Instead of your subconscious mind being in charge of your VDU, you can make your own dreams happen. This is known as lucid dreaming. You can decide what you want to dream about before you go to sleep and programme your mind to dream it; you can even ask your subconscious mind to provide answers to your life questions. Your dream world will respond by sending you messages encoded in symbolic images, and once you become accustomed to the language of your dreams you can begin to unravel them. You can enter another world, revel in its mystery and bring back to your waking life a new wisdom. We'll talk more about lucid dreaming on page 66.

your dreams are unique

You are the one and only person experiencing your dream. The dream is happening inside your mind and you alone are in the auditorium watching the big screen. Your dreams come from your subconscious mind, relaying back to you your own unique emotional state, level of well-being, and worries and concerns. Two people can have roughly the same dream, but the meaning will be different for each one of them. Your dream and its meaning are as unique as you are.

Imagine that your subconscious mind is your own internal personal assistant, working for you 24 hours a day, every day, and working for your highest good. Just like your PA, it brings to your attention – in the form of dreams – important information and messages that you need to attend to. As you sleep, it is working away, filing, sorting and throwing out useless clutter. One theory has it that if this process did not happen each night, the human brain would have to be 20 times its current size to store all the information it has accumulated. Just as your computer defragments documents and files, your subconscious mind is constantly clearing memory space in your brain.

So What Exactly Is a Dream?

dreams offer inspiration and creativity

The world of dreams has been a source of inspiration for creative people throughout the ages. Mozart, for example, is said to have woken from his sleep and transcribed passages of music that came to him in his dreams. Classical music has often been described as the music of the gods channelled through the medium of both night- and day-dreams.

Shakespeare used the imagery of the dream world in several of his plays, such as *A Midsummer Night's Dream* and, a great favourite of mine, *The Tempest*. *The Tempest* is set on a lost island, where the characters are marooned in swirling winds and sea mist. Magic, mystery and wonderment envelop each scene as the playwright leads us through the enchantment of the dream world: 'We are such stuff as dreams are made on.'

Another great classic, the book and then film *The Wizard of Oz,* is set in the dream world of Dorothy's mind. She travels down the yellow brick road and meets up with new friends, the Tin Man, who is looking for a heart; the Scarecrow, who would like a brain; and the Lion, who wants to find his courage. In fact each of these characters represents an inner aspect of Dorothy's character – aspects that she discovers as she goes on her dream journey in search of wisdom, courage and love. As you read the book or watch the film, you have no idea that Dorothy's adventure is actually a dream until the end when she wakes up. She asks where her friends are – thinking they are real people – and then comes to the realisation that she has been dreaming.

Among countless famous works based on dreams, some of the best known are *Alice in Wonderland;* the Narnia books, including *The Lion, the Witch and the Wardrobe;* and *Gulliver's Travels* – all literary works inspired by journeys through the mind-blowing extravaganza of the world of dreams.

Many classic horror movies make use of the blood-curdling images of nightmare. The film director Alfred Hitchcock had a genius for exposing human weaknesses and fears. His films, such as *Psycho* and *The Birds,* have you gripping the edge of your seat in terror, and recapture the true horror of your worst nightmare.

The next time you are embarking on a creative project, in whatever medium – performance, painting, drawing, music – try drawing your inspiration from any one of your dreams, even one of your nightmares, and feel the creativity flow.

a message from yourself to yourself

You dream every single night and, as you now know, that can be anything up to 10 times each night. You will not be able to recall all your dreams and it is not important that you do so either. The vast majority of them will be what I call clutter-clearing dreams. Your subconscious mind absorbs every feeling and thought that goes through your mind every day, many of which will be incidental and of little value to you. At night when you sleep, it begins the work of sifting though them all and expels the ones you don't need by way of nonsensical dreams.

These dreams you tend not to remember. But every now and then a dream will stand out and prey on your mind. A dream such as this has been sent from your subconscious mind to your conscious mind as a message. It may have been sent to help or guide you, or to prompt you to sort out a personal difficulty, or to warn you of a potential problem, or to make you aware of your deep fears and feelings. The possible reasons are endless.

Why Do We Dream?

We have already discussed the thousands of thoughts and feelings that go through our minds every day – it would be impossible to even begin to count how many. All our thoughts – without any conscious decision on our part – are stored away in the subconscious mind. We know this because during hypnosis it is possible to access every moment of a person's life in the most minute detail, including the emotions that went with each experience. Hypnosis can take us back to our point of birth and, some people believe, further still, to previous lifetimes.

Our thoughts and emotions are constantly being processed by the subconscious mind. It is as though the subconscious is a clearing house, sorting thoughts and feelings into those that are helpful and those that are of little significance. When a situation arises in your life that needs to be dealt with, your subconscious mind may send you a dream. The imagery within the dream will highlight your situation in a symbolic way and direct you towards the issue that needs to be addressed.

If you can't work out the message the first time around, your subconscious is likely to send another dream, containing the same message in a different form. It will keep on trying until you eventually get the message and act upon it. You can imagine the subconscious mind as a player in a game of charades. It will try all sorts of ways of communicating without words the message it wants you to get, until hopefully you come up with the correct answer.

Just understanding your dream is really not enough, because your subconscious wants you to do something about the situation at the root of it. Let's say you keep dreaming about an argument you had with a good friend that you really regret. The dreams will keep coming until you contact your friend to make things up. Once you've done that, the dreams will stop and almost invariably your subconscious mind will get to work on another important issue.

dreams can help you heal

It is a belief in the area of holistic healing that physical symptoms can be a result of dream messages that have been repeatedly ignored. The holistic approach to healing aims to discover the root cause of the problem and heal that instead of treating the symptoms alone.

Let me give you an example: let's say that you've started to develop a stomach ache and no matter what you take to try to settle it, after a few hours it just comes back. Of course, if you have a physical problem that persists, the first thing you should do is seek medical advice. Once you have taken any medical steps necessary to deal with your condition, you may want to look at it from a holistic point of view. In this approach you would try to discover *why* your stomach was hurting by looking not just at any physical symptoms but also at your whole lifestyle. For instance, could there be deep-seated feelings of hurt that you have been denying and 'stuffing down'? Is a situation or a person upsetting you? What or who could be making you feel 'sick to your stomach'?

If your difficult situation has been going on for months – or maybe even years – and your subconscious mind has failed to get your attention through dreams, it may try to get through to you in another way. Continued emotional hurt can cause your stomach to churn, eventually causing a build-up of bile and acid that can make you feel as if your stomach is tied up in knots. At last, your subconscious has attracted your attention but this time in a more flamboyant and painful way.

Consider where all your painful feelings actually go when you have been emotionally hurt. Often they land up in the body somewhere, and if they are not acknowledged and resolved, that's where they may stay. As a result you may experience vivid dreams – messages from your subconscious mind prompting you to deal with the problem. This could be by way of talking, sharing your feelings with someone or confronting the issue. Whatever method you choose, facing your difficult feelings head on will often help to make you feel better. If you can deal with the root cause of your problem, you are much more likely to be able to get rid of your stomach ache permanently rather than suffering a recurring problem.

collective dreams

Throughout ancient history, human beings have evolved at a more or less uniform rate all over the world, learning to walk, use tools, develop language and build civilisations in more or less the same period of time as each other. Nevertheless, different races developed completely in isolation, and it was not until people began to build boats and travel longer distances that they discovered that other lands and races existed. So how is it that peoples who had never met – and indeed didn't even know of each other's existence – were developing and doing the same things at the same time?

One well-known theory for this universal development was put forward by Carl Gustav Jung. Jung identified something that became known as the collective unconscious. He suggested that we human beings are able to connect through our dream world, and that thus we communicate important developmental knowledge. This is one possible – and rather magical – explanation of how, for example, the wheel was invented at the same time in quite different parts of the world. Have you ever noticed how several people will often start to have similar ideas at the same time? The renaissance period in history is a great example of this. During this time many amazingly gifted painters with radical new ideas became active – artists such as Michelangelo, Leonardo da Vinci, Rembrandt and many others. A similar thing happened in music during the period when Mozart, Bach and Beethoven, to name but a few, produced great classical works of music. World-changing inventions, too, have often been developed at the same time by different people living and working continents apart and with no knowledge of each other.

Several years ago a good friend of mine was writing and recording her first single; it was called 'I'm Automatic' and was released in the UK in the same week that the Pointer Sisters brought out a single with exactly the same title in the US. Neither artist was aware of the other, but even the music was similar. How could this be? After that I began to notice lots of other interesting coincidences – or were they? How often has this happened to you?

How Can We Learn from Our Dreams?

As we've already noted, there are rarely any spoken or written words in dreams; dream messages arrive encoded in their own special language.

It would be so much easier if you woke up in the morning and your subconscious mind had left you a text message telling you exactly what you need to do today, but what it actually leaves you is a set of images. You just have to learn to decipher this special language so that you can understand the message. Sometimes this will be very clear and straightforward, but often the message will be confusingly concealed among many images within your dream.

Nevertheless, understanding your dreams is not as difficult as it may at first appear, and once you have grasped the meaning of a few dreams you will soon become familiar with how your subconscious mind works. Interpreting your dreams will be easy and a great source of fun and inspiration.

learning to understand your subconscious

Let's imagine that your subconscious mind wants to tell you that you are working too hard at your studies and are very tired – you could do with a break, some time out, a holiday. Here are some images that might put over this message:

- A broken clock

- A clock whose hands are going backwards

- A beach scene, with someone lying asleep on a sun lounger and a group of people playing in the sea.

These are just a few of the more obvious examples, but now let's take this exercise further. Say you have still not understood the message. How could this message be conveyed in an even more vivid way?

- You are walking in the rain and feeling miserable, but across the road the sun is shining and everyone is sitting around enjoying beers and coffees; you can't cross the road because there is a huge wall running down the middle.

Still doesn't get your attention? Perhaps this could be your next dream:

- You are working in your bedroom at your desk and there are piles and piles of books that you have to study. Every time you finish one piece of work and put a book away, the pile in front of you has grown. You can hear everyone else in the house laughing at something on the TV – they are relaxing and enjoying themselves.

Let's say that you still haven't worked out what your dream is trying to get across to you. The images from your subconscious mind may start to become more forceful and take on a nightmarish quality:

- You are in a room from which you cannot escape.

- You are trapped underground and there is no light.

- You have broken out of a prison cell and are running away but the guards are after you and you know they will catch you and lock you up again.

Of course, this exercise could go on and on, as there is an infinite number of ways to get the same message across and your subconscious mind will keep on trying to catch your attention until, hopefully, you get the message.

putting knowledge into practice

The message is important, but it can only be helpful to you if you actually do something about it.

Let's say that at last you have worked out what the dream message is. Well, of course you know you are tired and you are also fully aware that your life has become a treadmill of work, work, work ... big deal! You know it would be great to have a holiday but you can't afford to let your work slip and anyway you haven't got any money to go on holiday. You may begin to ask what the point is of your subconscious mind sending you all these dreams about something you know already.

Well, maybe you did know all these things on one level, but perhaps you haven't really been letting yourself see that overworking is becoming a problem and that you need to deal with it. Often it's only when we're *deeply* aware that there is an issue we have to tackle that we really take it on board and look for a solution. So what can you do about this dream? Begin by thinking small. You don't need to start a revolution; minor changes can make a major impact. You'll probably be surprised at just how much effect a tiny change can have in your life. For example you could:

- Study with a friend to ease the monotony
- Allow yourself a couple of hours' break from your studies one evening a week just to relax
- Watch a good movie to escape for a while
- Take a whole night off and go out with some friends
- Plan a weekend away and stay with a friend

Any one of these actions is a positive way of dealing with overwork, and no matter how small the action you take is, you are acknowledging your dreams and trying to help yourself. Your subconscious mind will register this and you will start to feel generally happier. You will find that your dreams become much gentler and your sleep much more restful – that is until your subconscious mind has another important message for you to grasp of course.

Types of
Dream

There are many different types of dream, and each of them requires a slightly different perspective when it comes to understanding what it is about and how we can use it to good effect. In this chapter we're going to run through just a few of the main dream types that you may encounter.

nightmares

There is a scarcity of insightful literature on the subject of nightmares. I'm going to start with them here, because they are often feared and misunderstood. Unlike many people, I see them not simply as a horrible and terrifying experience but as a fascinating method of communication between our waking and sleeping minds. In fact if you view nightmares in this way – as your subconscious trying really hard to get in touch with your conscious mind – you'll probably begin to find them more fascinating than worrying.

Nightmares are often alarming and distressing, despite the fact that most make little sense to us once we wake up. Often, the most memorable thing about a nightmare is a confused feeling of terror or anxiety and a certain trepidation about going back to sleep in case the nightmare recurs.

Nightmares may be distressing, but evidence suggests that they are often nothing more than a kind of mental refuse collection, designed to clear the vast debris of thoughts and emotions that accumulates throughout the day. However, a vivid nightmare that you recall afterwards will almost certainly carry a message for you to unravel. The message itself is likely to be far less dramatic than the events in the nightmare, probably quite unthreatening, and perhaps even banal. It appears that sometimes the only way the subconscious mind can get your attention is by giving you a jolly good fright with a quality nightmare!

Of all dreams, nightmares are the best remembered and most fervently talked about. They tend to appear at very stressful times in our lives, and the teenage years are certainly stressful. Indeed, this is likely to be one of the most challenging periods of your life. Every aspect of your life is changing rapidly, and your abilities as a person are constantly being tested, socially as well as academically. You may fall in love for the first time, sit an apparently never-ending stream of exams, leave home to go on to further education, or face the nerve-wracking experience of a first important interview – just to name a few of the likely landmarks to come your way. You will regularly be faced with frightening decisions that appear to determine what you will end up doing for the rest of your life! Coupled with all these pressures is the fact that the teenage years are a time of immense hormonal upheaval, making your day-to-day existence an emotional roller coaster. So don't be surprised if you get a few nightmares!

If you're lucky, you can share your personal problems with your closest friends and family. Talking about your problems with people who care about you can, of course, be a great help. Nevertheless, to deal with each new day you probably put on a brave face to face the outside world – you have to in order to get yourself through. To the outside world you may appear to be confident, capable, coping admirably and getting on with your life, and often only you will know the true extent of your inner turmoil.

It is natural to try to push uncomfortable emotions away, to hide them deep down in the recesses of your subconscious mind. We all do this routinely, so that we don't have to deal with our emotions immediately. We may hope that they will stay buried indefinitely, or even better that they will just go away. But the subconscious mind knows better than to keep uncomfortable truths locked away – it is simply not good for you and can even make you physically ill.

The subconscious mind actively tries to free your buried thoughts by way of dreams. If you have been desperately trying to avoid a certain emotional situation or ignore a specific problem that is only going to get worse in time, your subconscious will start to conjure up vivid dreams to bring the issue right to the forefront of your attention. If you continue to be unaware of the messages contained within your dreams, your subconscious mind will respond by making your dreams even more vivid, furious and frequent. A nightmare is a sure way to grab your attention.

stressful situations can induce nightmares

Let's look at some everyday, apparently normal situations that can be the cause of considerable stress.

You are invited to a party ... great! But what are you going to wear? Sounds simple enough, but let's look at the emotions and thoughts that may accompany this scenario.

When you pick an outfit for a party, part of what you are doing is attempting to boost your self-esteem as much as you can so that you will feel confident and carefree in the presence of a group of people, many of whom you will not be familiar with. In the process you will look at yourself and evaluate how you appear. You may come to the unhappy conclusion that you are too fat or too ugly or maybe just 'totally un-cool'. Whatever form they take, some destructive thoughts will probably be going through your mind.

Let's stay on the same theme. So you eventually get yourself to the party and you start to think about how great everyone else looks. You are probably also feeling a little nervous and unsure of yourself. What if no one talks to you? What if no one fancies you? You may look as if you are joining in with everyone else and partying away, but that's not what you're feeling like inside.

Let's take the scenario a stage further and say that someone you fancy gives you the brush-off. You realise there's not a cat in hell's chance of the two of you getting it together. How does this make you feel? Not good enough? You may even come to the conclusion that there's something wrong with you. But no one could possibly guess how you are feeling because you look as though you are having a great time and you may even dismiss how you are feeling yourself.

Where do all those feelings that you are experiencing go? Well, they don't just go away; they are all stored in your subconscious mind. Your subconscious mind could be likened to a locker room. If you experience a particular feeling several times, the locker in which it is stored may get full up and will have to be emptied. Using this analogy, we can picture a mechanism whereby destructive emotions that we fail to deal with are released for processing into our dreams, sometimes in the form of a nightmare. What message might your nightmare try to communicate to you? In the party example above, it's likely that your nightmare would contain symbols of insecurity, worthlessness and rejection.

Let's look at another example of a stressful situation. It takes months of preparation for exams and weeks of tense waiting for the results, during which time all sorts of negative thoughts and depressing feelings may be going through your mind. Personally, I've suffered from every form of mental inadequacy known to man when preparing for exams. For example, there's hopelessness: 'I'll never finish reading this book in time – it's hopeless'; and helplessness: 'No matter how many times I read it, I still don't understand it!' Or you may feel that you are 'just not clever enough'. You may even question why you are bothering to take exams at all. Alternatively, you may fluctuate between day-dreams of passing your exams with the highest marks, and despair at the thought of failing miserably. What if all your friends pass their exams and you don't? You will be left behind, humiliated, and perhaps even mocked by your peers. What if you do pass? You may be worried that you will then have to deal with the daunting task of leaving home, finding somewhere new to live and making new friends. Even success is stressful!

When all these feelings are absorbed into your subconscious mind, what kind of dreams might result? Nightmares are often mirrors of your deep fears and insecurities; in this instance, perhaps your dreams would take the form of nightmarish representations of failure and perhaps humiliation. Remember, though, a dream of failure does not mean that you are going to fail your exams; it merely indicates that the possibility of this happening is something you are afraid of. By bringing this fear into your conscious awareness and facing it realistically, you will put a stop to your failure nightmares and will probably feel more confident all round.

common nightmare themes

While each dream is completely unique to the individual dreamer, nevertheless there are some symbols and images that turn up in many of our dreams. Let's now take a look at some of the common themes of nightmares.

monsters

A typical scenario in this nightmare might be that a terrifying monster is chasing you; however fast you run, it is still there behind you. You know that when it gets you it's going to kill you. Just before it catches you, you wake up screaming.

If this is one of your regular nightmares, try making a conscious effort to face your monster before going to sleep. The monster is likely to represent a facet of your life that you are repeatedly ignoring or even desperately avoiding. It is chasing you because it literally wants to grab your attention! In your waking state, try to imagine what the monster looks like and what is making it so angry with you. If you can picture the monster's face, is it as terrifying as you imagine?

Your monster could represent an emotion or cluster of emotions that you are either suppressing or failing to express sufficiently. Alternatively, it may represent a certain situation in your life that you are running away from. It may even be a part of your personality that you don't like and are trying your best to deny.

If the latter is the case, remember that it's normal to have 'negative' feelings such as anger, envy, jealousy and even hatred. You may feel bad about yourself for having these types of feelings and try to shut them away, but they are natural and can be expressed in a healthy way too. If you try to suppress negative feelings, they will surely come back to haunt you – perhaps in the form of monsters who inhabit your dreams.

Ewan's monster nightmare: *I'm walking down a dark alley which is cobbled and very narrow. I can hear the heavy footsteps of something behind me, but I'm too frightened to look back. I begin to walk faster, and then I start to run, but the thing is still following me. I can tell by the sound that whatever it is, it isn't human. I catch sight of its shadow; it's huge and grotesque and full of evil, and it's going to kill me. I wake up in a cold sweat and am too frightened to go back to sleep.*

Interpretation: Ewan was the captain of a college football team. He had found himself becoming increasingly furious with Tom, one of his team mates. Tom was a great player but he had begun to let the team down by failing to turn up for matches each Saturday. Every time Tom failed to turn up, Ewan found himself in the awkward position of having to find a replacement at the last minute. The team never played as well without Tom. Ewan was determined not to make a big deal of Tom's behaviour because he didn't want to upset the rest of the team by arguing with Tom. At the same time, however, he wanted to tell Tom what he thought of him. He was always meaning to do this, but he kept putting it off until another day. He simply didn't think he could speak to Tom without losing his temper, and this was something he really did not want to do. Every Friday night, Ewan would have a nightmare in which a terrifying monster was chasing him. Ewan was angry with Tom but he wasn't expressing it. Instead, his anger was being pushed deeper and deeper into his subconscious mind, where it bubbled away waiting to be dealt with. So Ewan's subconscious began trying to make contact with his conscious mind through nightmares. Let's imagine what the monster in his nightmare might say to him if he stopped to listen to it:

> I'm furious because you keep ignoring me. This is really frustrating. I keep trying to catch up with you so that I can tell you to do something about this situation with Tom, and then I can be at peace. I keep coming to you in your dreams and trying to get your attention but you keep running away and ignoring me. I keep making myself bigger and more frightening so you will notice me, but the bigger and louder I become, the faster you run.

Resolution: Once Ewan had figured out that the monster in his recurring nightmare represented his own anger and was only trying to make him aware of this, he felt that at last he could deal with the situation. Eventually, Ewan faced Tom and told him that he was no longer on the football team. He added that he had been feeling angry and frustrated with Tom for some time and that Tom had let the whole side down. Tom innocently asked, 'Why didn't you tell me this before; I didn't think it mattered – it just gives someone else the chance to play!' Ewan dealt with his monster and learned that, within reason, he needed to say what he thought when he thought it. In future, he wouldn't wait for his monsters to come and get him.

A lesson to be learned here is that monsters are usually of your own making and are simply a part of yourself wanting to be expressed. If you find a monster in your dreams, try to look at it and imagine what it would say to you. Ask yourself where in your waking life you are ignoring an emotion that is crying out for your attention.

being chased

This is a very common dream theme and can have a very simple explanation. In some cases this dream may have little or no meaning, because we all tend to dream about being chased just before waking up. It could be as simple as your subconscious mind getting you ready to wake up. If your dream feels more significant than that, ask yourself what it is that you are running away from in your waking life. When you discover what that is, make sure you take steps to deal with this issue.

falling

A dream in which you have the sensation of falling may have a very simple explanation, as we tend to dream that we are falling very early on in the sleep cycle – when we are just falling asleep. This may be a symbol of leaving the waking state and falling into the unconscious state of sleep. If your dream feels more significant, consider what it is in your waking life that you need to let go of. What is making you feel out of control? Are you falling for someone, or are you afraid of falling in love?

paralysis

Again, there may be a very simple explanation for the theme of paralysis in dreaming. As we have already seen, during the REM sleep phase, when dreams occur, the body is in fact unable to move (see page 19). Therefore you might very well dream that you are paralysed, simply because in fact you are. However, if your dream feels more significant than that, it could be carrying an important message from your subconscious mind. Take a look at your waking life and

Types of Dream

consider in which areas you feel stuck or unable to move. Is there a situation or a relationship that is grid-locked and going nowhere? Is this making you feel helpless and unable to move forwards?

🌿 **Chantelle's dream:** *It's very dark and I'm very frightened. I'm trying to walk but I can't; it feels as if my legs are caught in something and I can't move. In front of me is a crucifix and it starts to grow. On it is a woman. She has her hands nailed and they're bleeding. Her feet are also nailed, and there's blood and gore everywhere. It's terrifying. I can't do anything to help her because I can't move. I don't know who she is. I wake up screaming with fright.*

🌿 **Interpretation:** Chantelle did not at first recognise the woman on the crucifix in her nightmare, but when we discussed this dream together we came to the conclusion that in fact she represents Chantelle's mother. At the time of the nightmare Chantelle's mother was working hard and struggling to take care of her family at the same time. All in all, she was not coping very well. As the eldest child in the family, Chantelle really wanted to help her mum, but she felt that, at the age of 12, there was nothing she could do – she was far too young. This sense of helplessness manifested itself in her nightmare, in which she experienced herself as stuck and unable to move.

🌿 **Resolution:** Chantelle talked through her concerns with her mum and found that there were in fact things she could do at home to help to make life easier for her mum.

sinking

Sinking dreams may indicate that in some area of your waking life you feel as if you are going under. Is there an area of your life where you feel that you are sinking or where you are finding it difficult to make any progress? Ask yourself if you are working too hard or taking too much on. Could it be that another person is 'dragging you down'? Is there a situation that you know is hopeless and that is giving you 'that sinking feeling'? Once you work out what it is, then you can start to take positive action. The message of this nightmare may be that you should stop working so hard and just take things a bit easier, at the same time asking for help if possible.

naked in public

This is a very common dream theme and has nothing to do with sexuality. This sort of nightmare may be connected with feeling exposed, vulnerable and raw, or even feeling on show. Ask yourself if you have said or done something in your waking life that you are feeling foolish about. Has someone or something made you feel stupid? Have you been the focal point of other people's ridicule and has this left you feeling exposed and 'naked'? Have you been stressing about an event that is due to happen, such as a performance or a speech that you have to give – a situation where you are going to be on show?

On the other hand, you might dream about being naked and on show and feel really good about it. This type of dream can be a positive message of feeling free and confident in yourself.

> **Joanna's dream:** *I'm walking through the school gates and everyone is looking at me, but I don't know why. They're laughing and making fun of me. It's just horrible. I'm standing there all alone and I've got no idea why they're doing this to me – until I took a look at myself. I've got no clothes on at all – I'm starkers! I've got my school bag over my shoulder and I'm trying hopelessly to cover myself up with it. It's awful. I wake up in a cold sweat.*

Types of Dream

✽ **Interpretation:** Joanna had written an essay about her school holidays, and her teacher was so impressed that she asked Joanna to read it out to the class the following day. Joanna felt very embarrassed and really did not want to do this at all. She felt that her essay was too private and she didn't want her friends to hear it, as she had written things about them too. Joanna is the type of girl who would rather sit quietly at the back of the classroom and keep her thoughts to herself. At the same time she did not want to let her teacher down. The dream was highlighting her feelings of insecurity and her sense that by reading her essay she would be giving too much of herself away.

✽ **Resolution:** Joanna plucked up the courage to discuss her fears with her teacher. They agreed that Joanna's teacher would read out the essay but would not say who had written it. This was an arrangement that Joanna felt comfortable with.

being laughed at

A nightmare in which people are laughing at you and ridiculing you can make you feel pitifully stupid and ashamed. It is possible that this dream indicates that someone in your life is having a laugh at your expense; however, another interpretation is more likely. This type of nightmare often suggests that you should not take yourself so seriously and that maybe you should try to see the lighter side of life a bit more. Consider where in your waking life you are taking things too seriously. Do you feel that there are areas in your life where you could have more fun? See if there are ways in which you can lighten up a little.

teeth falling out

Imagine the sensation of grinding your teeth. Inside your mouth, your teeth feel larger than they should be. They are growing and growing. You begin to grind your jaw harder to give your teeth more room, but there is no room. They start to pull out their own roots and come loose. You can hear the grinding noise of bone and feel the raw flesh. Your mouth is full of crumbling teeth and you have to open your jaw wide. When you do so, blood and broken teeth fall out. You scream, and thankfully wake up. Exhausted, you slowly come round and pluck up the courage to check your mouth – all teeth in order. Phew, thank goodness, everything is all right. It was only a dream after all!

This is such a dreadful dream and yet is surprisingly common. There are several opinions about what it means, but I feel that this type of dream is related to frustration – possibly sexual frustration. Frustration is pent-up energy that has no means of escape, and it's pretty obvious how grinding your teeth could represent this feeling. Consider if there is a situation in your life that is making you feel frustrated.

Alternatively, think about teeth as part of your body image. Your beaming smile is a significant part of your appearance and an important factor in how other people see you. Consider whether there is an area in your waking life where your image is falling apart and crumbling.

being lost

If you experience a nightmare in which you are lost, consider where a sense of lostness could also be happening in your waking life. Is there an area in your life where you are not sure which way to turn, where to go or what to do? Have you lost your direction in life?

Harriet's dream: *I am waiting for a train at the station. I'm sitting at a white table, and on the table are a cup, a saucer and a lollipop. I make them all levitate, which feels amazing. I get on the train with my parents. We are all sitting together, but when the train stops at the next station my mum and dad get off and leave me behind. I am upset and call out to them but they keep walking away from me. Then I'm in this dark tunnel. I try to walk but it's so dark everywhere I turn. I don't know where I am or how to get back. I call my mum on my mobile, but she tells me that she and my dad don't want me any more. The credit runs out on my mobile. I'm crying and hysterical and I just feel so lost and frightened.*

※ **Interpretation:** Harriet was sitting exams and was under a lot of pressure to do well. She also knew that if she passed them as expected, life would change big time. She was panicking about the whole situation. Nevertheless, there are several positive messages within her frightening nightmare. The train in her dream represents her journey in life. Her parents travel with her some of the way and then leave. Despite her fear at being abandoned by them, the strange experience of levitating the cups and saucers seems to be telling her that she will manage just fine without them. The implication is that she is in control and can make anything happen.

※ **Resolution:** Harriet's sense of panic and feeling of being lost were genuine emotions, which she was able to discuss with her parents. Talking with them about her dream made her feel much better. They told her they would always be there for her and support her when she needed them, which is just what she wanted to hear, even though she knew it all along. She just needed reassurance.

being trapped

If you have a nightmare in which you are trapped, look to your waking life and try to find a parallel. Consider whether there is a situation that is making you feel trapped and locked in. Could there be a relationship that is suffocating you and stopping you moving forward with your life? Is there a part of your life that feels as if it has come to a dead end? If you discover an area where you are feeling trapped, start to do something about it. Make changes that allow you to move forward positively and get on with your life.

drowning

Drowning dreams can be very distressing and cause acute panic. One possible practical cause of them is having something over your face, so make sure that your duvet isn't pulled up over your head and suffocating you. As you will realise by now, the outside world can filter through into your dreams.

If you're not suffocating under your duvet, consider areas of your life where you are struggling to cope, where you feel that you are being overwhelmed. Have you taken on too much work? Does it feel as if things are getting on top of you?

Water is usually linked to emotion and it may be that you are not coping with an emotional situation. Is your heart full of sorrow? Do you feel the need to cry about something? Has something become too much to bear and started overwhelming you?

When you have this type of dream, it is wise to pay attention. Such a striking image is a very strong call to sit up and take notice – and, more importantly, to take steps to resolve the situation. Try to discover what it is in your waking life that is making you feel like this, and be brave enough to ask for help if necessary.

being killed

First of all, let me reassure you that no matter how horrible it feels to have this sort of nightmare, it does not mean that you are going to die. This dramatic nightmare is letting you know that there is something in your life you need to let go of. This could be a friendship or a relationship that is coming to an end. It could be an unhelpful feeling, such as love for someone that is unrequited, or a behavioural trait that you might be better off without, for example smoking. A dream about being killed can also indicate that a new phase in your life is about to start and that you have to let go of the present situation – examples might be a move to a new house or a change of school.

If you have recently thought about making a life change, this nightmare may be a message of support and encouragement to let go of the past. Though alarming, this nightmare is usually positive. Your death in the dream is symbolic of the end of one phase of your life and, more importantly, signifies the beginning of something new.

death

Dreaming of death, especially your own death or the death of someone you love, can be very frightening. This is particularly so because in our culture we aren't comfortable with talking about and dealing with dying. Death is a process of life that we have come to dread because it is looked upon as an ending. In other cultures, however, death is regarded as only a stage in the journey, just as in winter nature appears to die, only to be reborn again in the spring.

In line with this wisdom, a nightmare about death does not suggest that you are about to die, but that something is about to be born – many ancient books on dreams give this interpretation. This nightmare highlights a change in your life. This change may be very significant, such as a new relationship, a new job, a move to a new school or college or leaving childhood behind to become an adult.

Take a look at your waking life and try to discover what is about to change and what you are leaving behind. This could be a practical change, but it could just as well be an emotional one – perhaps there is an emotion that you would benefit from letting go of, for example, anger that you have been harbouring for too long.

This nightmare, no matter how scary it may seem, is actually a message of support and encouragement to go along with this change.

Christine's dream: *I am watching a funeral. As the hearse drives by me in the street I look at the coffin and see a young girl who I vaguely recognise ... To my horror I realise that it's me. Behind my coffin are lots of my relatives crying. I'm screaming at them and telling them that I'm alive. I panic and run up and down, but they can't see me or hear me. The air is filled with floating balloons, the ones that you have at parties.*

Interpretation: Christine had decided to get married instead of going on to university. Even though it was a big decision to make, she was sure it was what she wanted to do, but her family was angry and upset with her. Christine was saying goodbye to her old way of life, one to which she would never return. A new life was waiting for her. The balloons were a sign of future happiness and of something to celebrate.

🌿 **Resolution:** Although her nightmare was very frightening at the time, once Christine had worked out its meaning she was able to talk to her parents and make it up with them. She decided to carry on with her studies too. The wedding went ahead and was a joyful day.

digging the meaning out of nightmares

Of course nightmares are frightening – that is their nature – but try to look at the emotions that may be buried underneath the fear. If all you can find really is fear, then ask yourself what you are frightened of in your waking life at the moment and consider whether this could be the source of your nightmares.

To help you to pinpoint other messages in your nightmares, take a serious look at your general situation in life. Consider whether anything unusual, outstanding or different has happened in the last few days that could be disturbing you. Is there an ongoing situation in your life that is screaming for your attention and that you should to be dealing with? Is there a situation that will arise in the near future that you are feeling apprehensive about? Jot down as much as you can about your current situation and attempt to work out how you are truly feeling – really feeling – deep down inside, because your nightmare is trying to reveal this to you.

Is nothing registering? Can you make no sense of your nightmare at all? If so, don't have nightmares about it! If you are unable to work out the message in your nightmare, then your subconscious mind will send you another one until you manage to! It may send you several nightmares, each one apparently different at first glance. When you look more closely, however, you will see that they are all just different ways of attracting your attention to the same issue. No matter how unpleasant your nightmares are, make an effort to understand them, because the sooner you do, the sooner they will stop.

nightmares are positive

Your subconscious mind really is your friend and is working with your best interests at heart. It is not out to get you, even though it may feel like that when you wake up terrified from a nightmare. It is trying to communicate with you in order to make your life better.

So what is the point, you may ask, of your subconscious mind making you aware of all those uncomfortable emotions? The answer is, to prompt you to learn how to deal with your fears and insecurities in ways that are supportive rather than destructive.

By taking heed of your nightmares you might discover, for example, that rather than bottling things up, it's more constructive to talk to people who care about you and seek appropriate advice. Your dreams are guiding tools that can actually help you at pivotal stages of your life. Learning to understand them will make you a much better and happier person, and in the long term everyone else will benefit too.

Having said all that, it's true that nightmares can sometimes be totally nonsensical and it may be impossible to work out any theme or purpose to them at all. Even so, they still act to express your emotions in a very dramatic way, even if all you are aware of when you wake up is that you were frightened. Whether you are aware of these emotions or not, they are still being released and expelled in a way that is not harmful to you or to anyone else, rather than festering away inside you, which can be unhealthy.

As a final note, nightmares can be distressing. If they recur over a period of time and you feel unable to deal with them, please talk to a responsible adult or seek professional advice.

warning dreams

This type of dream usually comes to you as a clear and obvious message. A warning dream is similar to a premonition dream, but in the case of the warning dream you can prevent the dreamed-of event from happening. If, however, you do not take heed of the dream, there is a possibility that the events in it may indeed happen. A warning dream is just that, a warning, and it gives you the opportunity to act upon that warning. These are dreams that you will immediately feel you have to do something about, for your own safety and the safety of those around you. When you wake up from a warning dream you will know exactly what it is that you have to do, such as:

- Turn off the lights before you go out of the house
- Remember to lock the house doors
- Keep an eye on your bag
- Check that your pets are safe
- Make an important phone call
- Keep a promise you have made
- Do something you had forgotten about
- Go to the doctor's

Here is an example of that kind of dream:

- **Clare's dream:** *I am sitting in a car with my friend, and my bag is on the backseat. We are talking and laughing, and when I turn round my handbag is gone – and more importantly the contents.*

- **Interpretation:** Clare woke up just knowing that the dream was a warning and that she had to keep an eye on her bag. In fact, the very next day her friend had her bag stolen, which made Clare feel really odd for a long time.

- **Resolution:** Clare had a sense of knowing that this dream came to her for a reason. After having it she became much more careful with all her belongings.

recurring dreams

A recurring dream is one that follows a certain specific sequence of events and that comes back to you time and time again. If you have a recurring dream, it is likely that your subconscious mind is desperately trying to get an important message through to you. The dream will stop recurring when you have worked out what it means.

Sometimes people who have suffered great trauma re-live their experiences again and again in their dreams. This phenomenon is stress-related and does not hold any message as such from the subconscious mind; it is simply an expression of deep pain and anguish. Time and counselling can help heal this wounded mind. Survivors of all kinds of terror, road accidents, train crashes and aeroplane disasters may possibly suffer these disturbing dreams.

The other type of recurring dream will come to you many times throughout your life and can act as a great guide to your emotional state during various important periods. The dream will have a similar theme and overall appearance each time it comes to you, but there will be slight differences; in these differences are the clues as to your current situation.

Each time my own recurring dream comes to me I feel it is reminding me that I have passed another milestone in my life. It comes to me every few years and mirrors my emotional state at the time. When I have this dream I know that change is imminent and that it is time to take another step forward in my life.

The following is a recurring dream of mine. It varies slightly every time I dream it, but the overall storyline is always the same.

🌿 **Anna's dream – one:** *I am about to dive into water. I take a huge leap off the diving board and elaborately dive into the water below. Sometimes this is at the swimming baths, sometimes at the seaside. When I was in my late teens, this dream became a nightmare. I would dive into the water and my head would hit the bottom of the pool, or I would only manage to swim a couple of strokes before I hit the concrete side, almost knocking myself out. The pool was always too small and constricting.*

🌿 **Interpretation:** Using this dream I can always work out what state my life is in by looking at what happens when I hit the water. My teenage nightmare was clearly showing me that my life at that time was too restrictive and confining. I was not doing what I wanted to do but what I thought I should be doing for other people's sake.

🌿 **Resolution:** I needed to expand, to make my life and my world bigger. I had to take some concrete steps to make things happen.

🌿 **Anna's dream – two:** *At another point in my life the dream returned. This time when I dived into the water I kept on going down and down, and when I tried to come up for air I couldn't get to the surface. I knew I was going to drown.*

🌿 **Interpretation:** When I woke up I knew immediately that something in my life was wrong. It didn't take me long to work out that the feeling in the dream was exactly the same one that I felt in my current job, where I was clearly 'out of my depth'. I was getting deeply involved in it even though I knew it was not right for me.

🌿 **Resolution:** The dream brought me to my senses and I left the job.

🌿 **Anna's dream – three:** *Some time later, when I felt that I had got my life back on the right course, the dream came back. This time, however, as I dived into a blue lagoon I was swimming at full stretch and felt incredibly happy playing and cavorting in the water.*

🌿 **Interpretation:** The dream was telling me that I was content and fulfilled and at last my life was on the right track.

🌿 **Resolution:** Relax and enjoy!

As you can see, recurring dreams can be very helpful, so look out for them. Once you have worked out what your recurring dream means, it can help you many times throughout your life and teach you a lot about yourself.

premonition dreams

A premonition is a sense of knowing that some event that you see in your mind's eye or have a sixth sense of will happen at some point in the future. Premonitions do not come only through dreams but can also arrive in the form of visions. You may have had premonitions yourself, and if you haven't yet, it's likely that you will experience one at some time during your life.

When you have had a premonition dream, you will wake up with an inner certainty that a particular event – good or bad – is about to happen. You may tell someone about your premonition, but whether you do or not, when the event does eventually happen you will have the feeling 'I knew that was going to happen'.

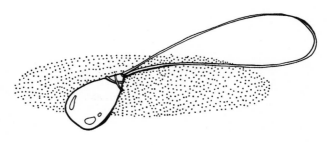

🌿 **Nicola's dream:** *I had this dream when I was a little girl and it has stayed in my memory for a long, long time. I was walking in a hillside village, and in the centre was a large square. At the centre of the square was an old water pump, and the road was made up of tiny cobbles in a circular pattern. I was drinking water from the pump. As I looked up, the sun was glaring in my eyes and I could just see a row of tall white houses not too far away. It looked like somewhere abroad.*

🌿 **Interpretation:** When I woke up, I knew with certainly that I would walk around the dream village for real one day.

🌿 **Resolution:** Many years later, when I was married, I went on holiday to Tuscany, in Italy, with my husband and daughter. We were staying in a rented villa and went into the village to buy food. I froze with amazement when I saw the little village square. It was the village in my dream, and there in the middle was the old water pump. My daughter went up to it and started pumping water in order to drink. It was her that I had seen in my dream, not myself. I recognised the cobbles and the white-painted houses close by, and I even knew how to get to the bread shop (to the surprise of my husband), which was down a tiny lane. I still to this day do not understand how or why this premonition came to me in my dream. Although a bit spooky, it was a wonderful and happy experience.

🌿 *Types of Dream*

predictive dreams

It is fairly unusual to have a predictive dream, unless of course you are a psychic, but they can and do happen, and when they do they can be very memorable, if disturbing at times. The prediction may be a clear and vivid image of something that is going to happen to you or to someone you know, but predictive dreams can also be on a much grander global scale. Your dream might predict an earthquake or an aeroplane disaster or the murder of a celebrity. If you do have this type of dream, you might want to share your prediction with someone, as this sort of dream can be distressing. There is little you can do about this type of dream, as what it predicts is beyond your own capabilities to change. Of course, not all predictions are nasty and frightening, but they can be.

※ **Samantha's dream:** *I dreamt that I fell in love with a boy called Andy – and I did!*

World disasters and the assassination of famous politicians or world leaders are often the stuff of predictive dreams. In ancient times such dreams were considered to be a serious means of looking into the future and a way of preparing for unexpected events and possible disasters. Predictive dreams were not only waited for but also actively encouraged and even expected.

The recorded documentation of predictive dreams is extensive. Over 400 years ago Michel de Nostradame, known to us now as Nostradamus, made many startling predictions. Throughout his life he was plagued by visions of death and destruction. His dreams foretold the rise of many great leaders and many events in the distant future. He predicted a great leader called Napoleon, warned the world about a man called Hitler, and described the French Revolution, the assassination of US President Kennedy, the development of the atomic bomb and the exploration of space. He even predicted the recent terrorist attack on the twin towers on September 11 and foretold of a Middle Eastern leader who would bring war and destruction. Centuries after his death, Nostradamus's predictions are still, incredibly, coming true today.

sexual dreams

Sex and sexuality can be a difficult and embarrassing subject at any time in your life but none more so than during the years when you and your body are preparing for adulthood. During your teens all hell is let loose with your hormones, and all sorts of weird and wonderful things start to happen to your body. At this time in your life especially, to have dreams of a sexual nature is, very reassuringly, natural.

As you leave behind the world of the child, you will become inquisitive about the mechanics of sex and at some point will want to experiment with the delights of the experience. However, because of the taboo on sexuality in our culture, you may often feel embarrassed by your sexual thoughts and uncomfortable with your sexuality. It takes time and maturity to really be able to celebrate your sexuality, but in the meantime remember that that squirming, uncomfortable, serious subject sex can also be a source of great pleasure and fun.

If I am perfectly honest, and I am going to be, I would expect that many of your dreams at this point in your life are of a sexual nature. How could they not be? The most basic drive within the animal kingdom is that of procreation of the species, and without it none of us would be here today. Add to this the fact that during REM sleep (the dream stage) the sexual organs of both males and females are stimulated, so to experience orgasm during your dreams is very common, especially for young men.

Our sexual drive is at its strongest when we are at the peak of physical condition, and that is during our teens and early twenties. Sex is a natural and healthy activity. However, the journey to discovering this can be an awkward and uncomfortable one, and you are likely at some point to experience such feelings as shame and guilt. These feelings will certainly be mirrored and expressed in your dream world.

When you dream you may experience the delirious delights of full sexual intercourse only to wake up feeling ashamed, guilty and embarrassed. Although sexual desire is normal and sex is a fundamental drive of all life, you may try to dismiss the whole issue in your head, coming to the conclusion that – whatever your dreams tell you – sex holds no place in your life right now. You may not be in a relationship, and you may have no interest in even having one. Your studies and your career may be the main thrust of your life right now, but whether you like it or not your sex drive will be there, and will probably emerge at some point in your dream world.

Though there are many sexual themes, the most common sexual dreams are actually reflections of sexual frustration. Whatever the nature of your dreams, the following are some of the sexual symbols that may appear in them:

- **Phallic symbols:** Poles, hosepipes, fountains, bananas, seeds, rams, goats, rabbits – plus any symbols that remind you of the penis and fornication, such as red sports cars or pillar boxes

- **Vagina symbols:** Ripe fruit, peaches, figs, melons, pillows, purses, dark holes, red fabrics, lips – and any other image that reminds you of the vulva

Here is an example of a dream with a very obvious sexual content!

- **Sandy's dream:** *I am walking down the path to my mum and dad's old house. Next thing, I am in their bedroom and in walks this hunk of a guy who is drop-dead gorgeous – he has a six-pack to die for. We start 'making love' – would be a very polite way to put it. Just then my mum walks in and says 'hi'. She walks over to her wardrobe and puts on a pair of new shoes that are yellow plastic and walks out of the room. When I wake up I can't get the dream out of my head. I don't say anything to my mum. I am s-o-o-o-o embarrassed.*

- **Interpretation:** Sandy is coming to terms with her sexuality and also her independence. In the dream her mother takes no notice of the sexual activity; this is telling Sandy that her mum acknowledges her womanhood. (It does not mean that she would accept wild sexual behaviour in real life, and this is not what the dream is about.) The yellow plastic shoes are a wonderful image. Shoes are a symbol of moving forward, yellow is the colour of joy and intelligence, and plastic is a sure sign of having fun. This dream is very positive even though Sandy found it embarrassing.

※ **Resolution:** Although Sandy was initially ashamed of this dream, she came to see that it was a natural expression of her sexual drive and just indicated that her sexual feelings were developing in a perfectly normal way.

lucid dreams

If you become aware during your dream that you are dreaming, you have entered the exhilarating state of lucid dreaming. The beauty of lucid dreaming is that you can now take control of your dream. Once you have mastered this art, your dream adventures will be endless. You can fly, visit different countries, go back in time, and turn your monsters into fluffy bunny rabbits.

It is possible, with practice, to teach yourself to lucid dream. It takes time and patience, but it can bring a whole new dimension into your dream world. The following technique has been used to help people with problem dreams and recurring nightmares.

Imagine that you are back inside your nightmare and slowly you begin to realise that you are dreaming – you know that what you are experiencing is not real. If you practise this visualisation enough, the realisation that you are dreaming will begin to come to you actually in your nightmare. Once you reach this point, you can take control of the nightmare by thought alone and change it however you want. If there is a monster chasing you, you can change it into your own personal slave, or whatever else takes your fancy. Instead of a frightening experience over which you have no control, dreams can become your own in-built virtual reality system!

You can use lucid dreaming to meet up with other people too. During times of great hardship, such as war, when loved ones are often separated, people have sometimes arranged to meet up in their dreams. Some couples even arranged a certain time each night to meet up, regardless of where they were or how dreadful the circumstances. It was a way of feeling close at such fearful times.

> **Esther's dream:** I heard this story from a woman, Esther, who had been in a Jewish concentration camp in the Second World War. Each night she met up with her husband in her dreams. They would meet by a fallen oak tree close to their old home, a place where they used to meet as young lovers. They would sit together in their dream every single night and talk to each other. One night Esther visited the old oak tree in her dream and her husband didn't turn up – he never did again. She knew he had been killed.

Lucid dreaming is an amazing experience; however, I would add one note of caution. When you consciously take control of your dreams you are blocking out any messages being sent to you by your subconscious mind. These messages are an important means of communication and are sent to you for your guidance and protection. It would be wise to limit the practice of lucid dreaming so that your naturally occurring dreams can continue to communicate with you.

astral travel

Properly speaking, astral travel is not so much a type of dream as an out-of-body experience in which the spirit or soul leaves the body. Although the experience has a dreamlike quality, you are fully aware that it is real, and you are conscious of yourself as your soul slips away from your physical self.

Although some people do have spontaneous experiences of astral travelling, by and large it is a skilled art that can be cultivated by only a very few people. Those with a very advanced spiritual practice, such as yogis, can sometimes choose to go astral travelling at will. A person who can astral travel is sometimes called an avatar. The soul can travel to other planets and can visit any dimension. It can go back in time and forwards into the future, and it can also be in more than one place at a time.

Some people believe that Jesus was an avatar, as it is recorded that he often appeared to several people, especially the apostles, at the same time in different locations. Today there are several highly developed spiritual beings who are said to be avatars, able to manifest themselves anywhere at will. Sai Baba, the world-renowned guru and spiritual master, is one of them. He is often reported to appear to people in times of great need even though he never leaves his ashram in India, where he lives with his followers.

The concept of astral travelling may be difficult for those of us who haven't experienced it to fully understand or accept. However, if we believe that it is possible, it certainly suggests that the soul can exist without the body, and therefore life after death becomes a distinct possibility.

※ **Olivia's dream:** *I was leaving school and wanted to get a job as a veterinary assistant. It was what I really wanted to do more than anything else in my life, and I tried everything I could to get the local vets' surgery to interview me. I wrote to them, called in, and telephoned several times, but the surgery was always busy and I never got any response. I did know who the head vet was, as I had taken my dog to him a few times. One night as I went to sleep I thought to myself, 'Well,* *if can't get to meet him in real life, I am going to meet him in my dreams.*

During my sleep I became aware that I was leaving my body. There I stood looking right down at myself lying in the bed. My 'spirit self' – that's the only way I can describe it – walked away, and the next thing I remember is sitting on the vet's bed talking to him. We had a great conversation and I told him how much I wanted to join his team and work with animals. Then I found myself back at my bedside looking at myself still sleeping. It was really weird.

The following week I had a telephone call from the vets' surgery inviting me in for an interview with the head vet. The interview was really odd – it was as if we had met before. I was offered a job there and then.

I'm still not really sure what happened or how I did it. All I know is that I was so determined that I managed to get to meet the vet in my dream. I just know that I did.

wish-fulfilment dreams

Sometimes we yearn for something so much that it begins to appear in our dreams. It is as if our desires have been granted and we can experience the pleasure of having our wish come true even if – for now at least – it's only in our dream world.

Imagine that you have wanted to be an actor since you were a young child. You have thought about it and day-dreamed about it for years. The desire is so strong that it is now stored deep in your subconscious mind. Naturally, it starts to filter into your dream world. In your dreams the audience is hushed with anticipation as you walk out into the spotlight, ready to delight them with your performance. When you take your bow at the end of the show, there is a roar of applause, and you are called back for encore after encore. When you wake up from your sleep you feel on top of the world. You know that acting is truly what you want to do with your life – even if perhaps you are a little disappointed that your grand performance was, this time, only a dream.

day-dreams

Properly speaking, day-dreaming is, of course, rather different from the dreaming we do at night. However, I think it's worth mentioning day-dreams here because, although they are generally more under the control of our will than are night dreams, they still provide a means of communicating with the unconscious mind.

Day-dreaming is a very natural pastime and often happens without you even being aware of it. Your eyes glaze over, time stands still and wonderful visions of how your perfect life would be are played out in your mind's eye. Day-dreams are part of who you really are. They come from your inner magical core and can help to connect you with your life's path and your wildest dreams. They shine the light of where your spirit wants to go, filling you with hope that what you are imagining will one day come true. I believe that day-dreams are vital in our lives and are the key to future fulfilment. Without them life would have no meaning and no purpose. If only day-dreaming were compulsory and we could officially dedicate a couple of hours to it each week! I'm sure the world would be a much happier place.

Later in this book I will be recommending that you set up a dream diary, dedicating half of it to your day-dreams. Write down the images that come into your head – yes, even the romantic and saucy ones. Do make sure that you keep this treasured book somewhere very private so that no one else can sneak a look – it spoils the magic!

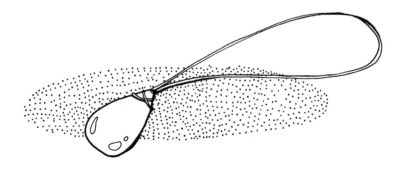

Types of Dream

By writing down your day-dreams over a period of time you will discover a lot about yourself – your likes and dislikes, your ambitions, your needs and your desires. Day-dream big – as big as you can – there are no restrictions. Let your imagination go wild; don't limit yourself. At least in your day-dreams you can have exactly what you want, and, who knows, in years to come you just may be amazed at how many of your day-dreams have actually come true!

Just look at this example by Neil Alden Armstrong. He was born in 1930 and – for those of you whose history is a bit rusty – was the first man to set foot on the moon, in July 1969.

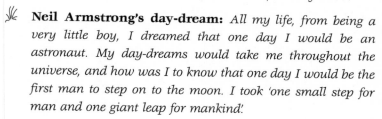 **Neil Armstrong's day-dream:** *All my life, from being a very little boy, I dreamed that one day I would be an astronaut. My day-dreams would take me throughout the universe, and how was I to know that one day I would be the first man to step on to the moon. I took 'one small step for man and one giant leap for mankind'.*

Dream Themes

In this chapter we will take a more in-depth look at some of the many common dream themes. Dream interpretation is, of course, always subjective; there are always several possible ways to interpret a given theme occurring in a dream. The suggestions here are guidelines only, but represent the most common explanations. Your own dream and its meaning are unique, but often you will be able to identify with a particular suggestion to some degree. No matter what the interpretation given in this book, your own feelings and instincts should always be considered carefully and respected, as they will help you discover with the greatest certainty the messages carried within your dreams.

Although dream themes tend to inter-relate, I have divided them into four main categories:

- **Natural things:** Water, fire, earth and air; weather, nature, animals and other creatures; mythological figures

- **Life concepts:** Birth and death, flying, falling, being chased, the toilet, sexuality, images of the body, celebrities, food and drink

- **Objects and activities:** Your home and other buildings, cars and status symbols, means of transport, sport

- **Abstract themes:** Colours, cartoon images, numbers, horoscopes

natural things

This first section deals with anything to do with nature, from trees to plants and animals to weather systems to mountains – and even dinosaurs! Basically, it includes anything you'd expect to find on the nature bit of the Discovery Channel!

water themes

Cocooned within the safety of your mother's womb, you are protected, nurtured and comforted as you float within your sheltered environment waiting to be born. In the dream world water has a feminine quality and represents the emotions. Sailors confer femininity upon the sea by referring to it as 'she', in the same way that they do with ships. Water is the most basic necessity for life itself; without water we cannot survive. Throughout history water has been used for ritual cleansing and purification, holy water being used to clear away negativity and evil forces.

Today, in the rich countries of the world, we take our water supply for granted: turn on the tap and there it is. This is a recent luxury; only 100 years or so ago, good, clean, pure water was regarded as a valuable commodity in the West. Still today, in many parts of the world, clean drinking water is not readily available. It is therefore easy to understand why in Chinese culture water is a symbol of money and prosperity.

Water is the source of life, and if it is in some way present in a dream, it is always a significant factor in the dream's meaning.

the sea

The deep, magical, mysterious sea is often described as the mother of nature. Consider the image of the sea in your dream. Are you sailing on calm blue seas sipping champagne on a yacht or are you struggling against the elements on a leaking boat in a terrifying storm, certain that you are about to drown?

Work through the situation in your dream, paying particular attention to what feelings are present. Once you have done this, take a look at your waking life. Consider whether any of these feelings relates to your mother or to any other strong dominant female figure in your life, such as a teacher or boss. Are they supportive of you or are they trying to overpower you in some way?

Storms at sea can represent arguments, and tidal waves may suggest that somebody is trying to dominate your life. Alternatively, a sea dream of something serene, such as walking calmly by the seafront, could carry a meaning as simple as that you need a holiday.

Phil's dream: *I am walking on a beach and in the distance is a cave. It looks very dark and I don't want to go near it. The sky is blue and the sea is calm, but I sense that everything is changing. There's a rumbling noise that is getting louder and louder. A storm is brewing and, furthermore, a great tidal wave is swiftly approaching. The noise is deafening and the wave is thousands of feet high, towering above my head. I know it will kill me, and realise that my only option is to run into the cave to try to save myself.*

Interpretation: In working with Phil's dream we came to the conclusion that the sea represented his mother. He had always had a very stormy relationship with her, and recently they had argued over his girlfriend, who is represented in this dream by the cave. Phil's mother can sometimes be rather overbearing and demanding, and at times he has felt that she was overpowering him and trying to rule his life. Whenever he takes steps to find his own way in life his 'tidal wave' dream will occur.

𝕄 **Resolution:** This dream sent strong message to Phil that no matter what he decided to do in his life, his mother was always there in the background, attempting to take control of his affairs herself. He loved his mother, but he decided that he had to take steps to stop her interfering with his life.

rivers and streams

Flowing water, such as rivers or streams, represents the journey of your life. Ask yourself these questions. Where are you going? Is it an easy ride or are you being swept away? Does the journey feel safe? Is the water too fast or is it too slow? Are you travelling in the direction that you want to go? Are you in control or do you have to put your trust in the flow of the water? Are you just enjoying watching the river and letting the world go by? Is the river plentiful or is it parched? Are you trying to cross the river (which could imply a desire to change the direction of your life)? Are you simply glowing with happiness as you 'go with the flow'? Consider the feelings present and then look at the various aspects of your waking life to see how they may relate to the dream.

boats

Boats are vessels of support that carry you on the journey of life. They can represent your home, your family, your work or any other area in your life that provides security, safety and support. Is the vessel in your dream safe and reliable or is it flimsy and letting in water? Is it a vast ocean liner or is it a small, leaky rowing boat? Is your boat moving in the right direction? Is it going too slowly or not moving at all? Consider the answers to these questions and think about how they relate to your waking life.

fancy yachts and speedboats

If the boat in your dream projects an image that is exciting, competitive and high-speed, it has a different significance than do other boats. Yachts and speedboats are fun vessels that represent energy, daring and sexual prowess. Do any of these adjectives describe your waking life? If, on the other hand, your life is dull and uneventful, this type of dream could be suggesting that you take some risks and make your life more challenging; you need a bit more drama and excitement! Sailing these types of high-speed vessel requires that you be in complete control and demands a considerable amount of skill and determination. Is your dream suggesting that you need or desire to get in the driving seat of your life and prepare to enter the fast lane?

shipwreck

This is a dramatic dream image. Consider your waking life: do you feel as if your world is falling apart? Have you lost control of a situation and does it feel disastrous? More importantly, how are you going to survive? Do you drift onto shore in your dream? If so, the message here is one of hope; no matter how bad things seem, you will come through. There will be times in your life when it feels as if everything is crumbling around you, but be assured that everything happens for a reason. A dream such as this will often be distressing, but you will be surprised at how often seemingly disastrous situations eventually turn out to be a blessing in disguise. Do not be afraid to ask for help if you need it.

swimming

Where are you swimming? Is it in a crystal-clear ocean where you are having fun on holiday, or is it in a muddy river where you are desperately fighting for your life? Are your strokes strong and confident or are you feebly paddling away from the inevitable jaws of a monster shark? What are your emotions? Try to relate any feelings or sensations to your waking life to discover how your dream is trying to help you.

floating

Floating in water symbolises the feeling of being supported. Floating can often represent a yearning to be cocooned or protected, as in the warm, safe environment of your mother's womb. Are you finding your waking life so difficult and stressful that you are crying out for support and in need of safety and comfort? Or is it exactly the opposite?

waterfall
This mysterious magical source of water can often symbolise birth. This may not be an actual physical birth but could be a sudden development within your life that is fresh, alive and energised. It can also signify a period of carefree fun, enjoyment and happiness, or a wish coming true. It is not often in life that we get to stand under a waterfall and feel the immense, almost magically vibrant energy generated by millions of tons of water. It is a spectacular image that we often see in films – or in TV commercials for soaps and shampoos! Standing under a waterfall can represent an act of cleansing, of wiping the slate clean, and in so doing making way for a new phase in your life.

showering
Taking a shower cleanses the dirt out of your life in an invigorating and refreshing way. Are you feeling tired and jaded and in need of a new lease of life? Taking a shower can symbolise letting go of the old and getting yourself ready for something new.

having a bath
Are you pampering yourself in a candle-lit bath surrounded by luxurious oils and perfumes, or are you sitting in an old tin bath, feeling cold and miserable? Are you immersed in the hot water, happy, content and emotionally safe and secure? Is this how you feel in your waking life, or is it how you wish to feel? If you don't have this sense of safety and security, how can you bring it into your life?

jacuzzis
Jacuzzis have a strong sexual undertone. They are fun, hot, steamy, and bubbling with life and energy. Consider how these images relate to your waking life. Are you having fun, getting out and socialising enough? If not, consider where

your life has become too serious. Maybe it's time to relax a bit and be more light-hearted. Playing and splashing about in water is a great way to relax and bring back the childlike joy to your life. Perhaps you are bottling up sexual energy. If so, you could try some harmless flirting; this will help to release some of the frustration.

carrying water
Water is a precious life-giving and life-saving commodity. Ask yourself where in your life you need nourishment or nurturing. Is there an area of your life that you feel is being neglected?

lack of water
Is there a situation in your life that was once thriving but has since 'dried up'? It could be that a once strong, healthy relationship or friendship has fizzled out or even ended. This dream could signify that prompt attention and nurturing might still repair the relationship. Water also represents money. Does your dream relate to finances? Is it funds that have dried up? Are you going through hard times? On the other hand, it may be that you are actually physically dehydrated. If so, when you wake up, remember to have a drink!

leaks
Leaks signify a draining of energy or resources. Assess your waking life to pinpoint the problem. Is it money, time or emotional energy that you are wasting? What should you be conserving or using more sparingly? If the leak is one of emotional energy, it may be harder to identify. Look carefully at where you may be allowing your resources to be used up unwisely.

flooding
This type of dream may be making you aware that a situation in your life has become too much to bear and the dam is about to burst. A flood is a build-up of water that is suddenly released, and as water represents emotion, you could be experiencing a build-up of emotions that are about to gush

out. This dream could be asking you to let go and release all that pent-up energy. Do you need a good cry about something?

fire themes

Fire is another fundamental power of nature that supports and sustains life on our planet. Fire is not only destructive but also provides heat. The sun is a burning ball of fire and without its rays of heat and light, life on this planet could not exist. Fire comes out of the sky by way of lightning, and bursts out of the earth from volcanoes.

In early prehistoric times, human beings did not know how to make fire. Can you imagine life without heat? However did we discover that by rubbing two sticks together fire could be made? Whenever or however that happened, life must have changed significantly for the better.

In ancient times the campfire was a place to gather around with your kinsfolk, a meeting place providing warmth and heat for cooking. Even today a fireplace is still the focal point of any room. Of course, these days, with central heating, there is no longer any need for a hearth. I personally feel that this has taken away an ancient element of magic from our homes.

Our ancestors lit fires not just to fulfil the basic functions of heating and cooking but also as a ritual element in celebrations and ceremonies. Fires were also used as a method of communication; lit high on a hill a fire could pinpoint your whereabouts for others, announce success in battle, warn animals and unfriendly people away, and alert others of impending danger.

Before their lands were taken over by white people, Native Americans used to light a burning fire on a hillside to send messages and warnings. They even evolved a language consisting of smoke signals. By covering the fire with a blanket they could control the flow of the smoke and so make different smoke patterns in the sky.

Fire has also been used from the beginning of time to cremate the dead. When a body is fed into the flames, the soul is symbolically released into the realm of the gods. Cremation also has the practical function of preventing the spread of infection.

Rite of passage rituals use fire to symbolise the cleansing and destruction of the old in preparation for the new, such as the beginning of manhood or womanhood. To throw a treasured item into a fire can also signify a symbolic letting go, such as the end of a relationship. Magic spells often use the powerful element of fire to set an energy free or seal an intention. If you have a wish or a deep desire, try this ritual. Write your desire down on a piece of paper – be clear and say exactly what it is you are asking for. Fold the paper up and, without telling anyone what you have written, throw it into the burning fire. Let go of your dream, release it to the fire and allow the magic of the fire to take it into the ether and help make it come true.

In former times, alchemists used molten-hot fire to try to change the molecular structure of various substances and make gold. Molten-hot fires are still used today in forges for the production of steel, cast iron and other metals that we use for innumerable purposes. Farriers and blacksmiths are some of the oldest practitioners of this fire craft today, forging metal to make horseshoes and wrought iron goods.

Fire is, of course, hot, and if it features in your dreams it could be suggesting that you may get burned, either emotionally or physically. Fire also represents anger and rage, as well as love, lust, and hot steamy sex! – a cauldron of passions and desires of the heart. Fire is sometimes represented by deep red.

Dreams containing fire can have many, many different meanings; your task is to consider your dream and discover what the fire means to you. Let's delve a little more closely into some possible interpretations.

fires and bonfires

Consider the fire in your dream; is it contained or is it spiralling out of control? Now take a look at your emotions and ask the same question: are they under control or are you in danger of losing it?

The location of the fire can provide you with some important clues. If it's outside in a public place, it may be concerned with an issue in your life that is in some way public. If the fire is in a house, it could indicate a personal, private issue, something to do with you alone, or with you and your family or someone close to you.

Is the fire in danger of going out? If so, consider what or who in your life may be in urgent need of attention.

putting out a fire

Is something in your waking life spiralling out of control? Do you need to put an end to it? Is there a friendship or relationship that you no longer want to be part of?

Are you putting out the fire by urinating on it? If so, it's likely that you are angry with someone or something, and perhaps you are not dealing with your anger. If you are poking a fire, what are you trying to get to the bottom of? Your dream may be suggesting that you delve even further. Or are you meddling in another person's business?

fire as a warning message

Fire is deadly. Your dream may be warning you to keep your distance from something or someone who may indeed present danger to you if you get too close. If you are disturbed by the dream, then try your utmost to work it out. This kind of message is usually important. It may be a simple and direct warning to you about fire safety, such as being careful with matches, turning off electrical gadgets, etc. The dream might save your life.

smoke

There's no smoke without fire. What is it in your waking life that is smouldering away? It could be anger or a grudge against someone. Is it likely to spark up again? Is there trouble around the corner or an argument brewing? Smoke is also a screen and stops you seeing the whole picture. Is someone hiding something from you, or are you keeping a secret from someone else?

buildings on fire

What type of building is on fire? If it's an office block, your dream could be to do with work. If it's a school, maybe you're ready to leave your own school and would be happy for it to burn down – metaphorically speaking, of course! If it's a garden shed, your dream could be about a hobby you're neglecting. If you're dreaming of the Twin Towers or a similar building, you could be experiencing deep fears about survival. A dream in which a building or other structure is burning down to the ground indicates that something will soon be leaving your life and that it's time to move on. Perhaps a move is even long overdue.

cooking over fire

Is there a celebration coming up that many people will enjoy? Could it be that you are 'cooking up' something in secret? Cooking implies that you are making plans, putting together ideas and generally scheming. Your dream could be suggesting that you need to do some more market research before you steam ahead with your plans. Maybe you should dwell on them a bit longer, mull over your ideas, let the status quo stand for a while, and be patient while they cook.

barbecues

A barbecue dream signifies a message about seeking fun. It is probably telling you to be more spontaneous and not take things too seriously. What better way to have fun than by inviting some friends round for a barbecue and a raucous party?

walking into a fire

This is an ancient symbol that marks a rite of passage. It represents leaving behind the old and being cleansed by the fire in preparation for a new phase in your life. This could be in the form of a major life change such as entering manhood or womanhood, or becoming a mother or father for the first time. Ask yourself what major development in your life is just around the corner? You are possibly about to enter unknown territory, and the issue here is your ability to place your trust in life. A dream like this is often positive; it suggests that you are aware of imminent changes and ready to take the first steps towards them.

Roi's dream: *I am in this dark red bedroom. There is a four-poster bed and the whole room is throbbing and mysteriously threatening. At the far end of the room is a roaring fire, burning away in a large black marble fireplace. I go to lie on the bed, which is empty. I am all alone. From somewhere behind me hundreds of large black cockroaches appear and start scurrying past me, over the bed. They rush towards the fireplace and then jump into the fire – hundreds and thousands of them. I wasn't particularly frightened during my dream, but it gave me the creeps when I woke up.*

Interpretation: Roi had been a bit of a 'jack the lad' with the girls for a long time. He was popular guy, full of fun and a free spirit. Then something happened that no one thought possible: he fell in love. He proposed to his girlfriend, got engaged and at the time of the dream was planning the wedding. The dream represented not only his passion but also the fact that he was undergoing a life-changing rite of passage. The cockroaches represented his fears and concerns, which were released as the insects headed straight into the fire. Roi was leaving behind his old life and entering a new phase as a married man.

emotional fire

Is the fire in your dream really a fire in your heart? Emotions of the heart are often described with images of fire. Take a look at some of these well-known expressions relating to passion: 'holding a torch for someone', 'my heart's on fire', 'my love for you will always burn bright', 'I have a burning desire to ...'. In pop music, poetry, literature and other art forms the analogy of fire is frequently used to express our passionate desires.

sexual fire

'Come on baby light my fire'. Red, the colour of fire, is also associated with sex and sexuality – with the flush of lips and pulsating blood pumping through excited veins. A dream in which fire is obviously related to sex can be disturbing, but this is a very natural dream to have, especially so when you are young and discovering what love, lust and your own sexuality is all about.

If you have had this kind of dream, consider your attitude to sex. Is it something you find uncomfortable to deal with in your waking life? Do you think that sex is dirty and vulgar? Does the mere mention of the word make you feel ashamed, guilty or embarrassed? If indeed you do have these feelings, they are very likely to surface in your dreams. Be considerate and gentle towards yourself and understand that these dreams are normal and will not be so intense when you are more familiar with your own sexuality. If, on the other hand, you are very comfortable with issues around sex, burning dreams can be positive and encouraging, and may possibly contain an element of wish fulfilment.

If you can, talk about the subject of sex with your friends; have a laugh and a joke about it. This will help you feel more comfortable around sexual matters. Sex is, after all, the reason we are all here; without it no one would exist! Procreation of the species is a fundamental drive shared by all living creatures.

candles

Is there a situation in your life that is out of reach or in some way covered up, secret or hidden? This dream suggests that you should shed some light on this matter and investigate it further. Are you holding a flame for someone? Or are you keeping someone in the dark or being economical with the truth? A multitude of candles may be related to a ritual or ceremony, such as a birthday.

unstoppable fire

Fire can be a terrifyingly unstoppable force of nature; just think about the intensity of a bush fire surging forwards with its wild energy. A dream of this type of fire can symbolise your own drive, energy and ambition, and may be willing you into action. If you're feeling lacklustre and devoid of ambition, a dream like this may be trying to motivate and inspire you, arousing your creative energy.

earth themes

Dreaming about earth is sometimes disturbing, as it may entail being buried or sinking into mud. Such dreams may be indications that there is a situation in your life that is difficult to cope with and that you find overwhelming. It may be that just acknowledging this fact is enough to turn things around. If not, make sure you seek appropriate help from a friend, relative or professional.

On the other hand, earth is grounding – it is the secure foundation on which we walk. A dream about earth may therefore indicate that you are feeling secure, established, sure of yourself. The earth also feeds us, and as such is related to the maternal principle (we talk about 'mother earth'), so earth in your dreams may suggest that you are feeling nourished, nurtured and protected.

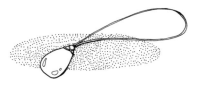

being buried

If you dream about being buried, examine every aspect of your life and consider what in it is burdensome to you. Do you feel as if everything is too much to bear? Is a situation overwhelming you or metaphorically burying you alive? If things become too difficult for you to cope with on your own, don't be afraid to talk to a responsible adult about it.

sinking into mud

Dreams about sinking into quicksand or mud may indicate that in some area of your life you feel as if you are going under. Perhaps you feel that there is no secure ground under your feet any more. Again, don't be afraid to ask for help from an older adult if you find that you can't cope with these feelings on your own.

earthquakes

If there is an earthquake in your dream, consider who or what in your life is making exciting ripples. Alternatively, ask yourself whether something is endangering the stability of your life. Do you need to make sure that your foundations are secure. Or does it feel as if your world is falling apart?

digging

If your hands are in the earth, your dream could be suggesting that you are trying to dig something up or get to the bottom of something. Having your hands in soil can be a grounding experience. The message within your dream may be that you should 'come to down to earth' for a while after a whirlwind period of exciting activity. If you are happily gardening in your dream, new plans for growth or expansion may be afoot that need your creative flair.

mountains

Mountains are, to say the least, significant features of nature, and when they appear in your dreams they will certainly represent an important aspect of your life. They symbolise your aims, goals and aspirations. A mountain can also represent your journey through life or a current obstacle that you are facing.

Are you climbing the mountain or are you trying to find a way around it? If you're climbing the mountain, is it an easy walk up or an uphill struggle? How does this relate to your waking life?

If you get to the top of the mountain in your dream, you may be feeling a sense of achievement – this is a sure sign of success. If you get to the top only to discover that there's another mountain ahead, your life has further challenges for you, which may lead to even greater success.

Do you get to the top of the mountain and fall over the edge? This suggests a fear of success or a concern about 'losing your grip' on a situation in your waking life.

air and weather

While we can survive a few days without water and a few weeks without food, we can only survive a few minutes without air. Of all the elements air is therefore the most essential to life.

Air may be associated with a certain distance from emotion or with an ivory-tower kind of intellectualism. It may also be connected with the freedom of flying – a fairly frequent theme of dreams.

In many dreams, the weather is a background feature that you pay little attention to. If, however, you do notice the weather, it will have some relevance to your waking life. In general, the weather in dreams represents how you are feeling. If the sun is shining, it denotes happiness and optimism in your life, but if the sky is full of big, dark, gloomy clouds, it signifies that your waking life is currently characterised by a mood of gloom and depression.

air

If you dream of being out in the open air, it may be that you are experiencing a positive sense of freedom in your life. If, on the other hand, you dream that you are suffocating, consider who or what is suffocating you in your life, perhaps by applying some form of pressure. And just a practical measure for any of you who have repeated dreams of suffocation: make sure that the duvet isn't over your face. Sounds obvious, I know, but it does happen ...

flying

Flying in your dreams can be an incredibly exhilarating experience. You are free from the physical constraints imposed in the real world, soaring high in the sky, as free as a bird, spying on the world below as you drift over it. Dream flying is wonderful – on several occasions, I have woken up only to be disappointed that my night-time flying session had ended!

If you have had a dream about flying, try to recall the feelings you experienced. Were you emotionally 'on top of the world'? Did you feel free, unshackled and excited? Ask yourself whether you recognise where you were flying. In the prelude to your flight, were you being chased? Did you suddenly take off just before being caught – like Harry Potter on his top-of-the-range Nimbus 2000 broomstick – and escape?

Flying in your dreams can signify that you feel a need for some form of escapism. On the other hand, if you are spending too much time up in the air with your head in the clouds, maybe you should come down to earth for a bit! Alternatively, flying may be a symbolic effort to stay optimistic about something potentially worrying – to rise above your concerns.

wind

Being blown around by the wind suggests a feeling of being out of control. The wind is a mighty element, and a powerful swirling wind in your dreams may signify a feeling of confusion and disorientation. But, on the other hand, a wind may also be blowing away the old and clearing the way for something new to come into your life.

hurricanes

This terrifying force of nature may signify that your life at this moment is really out of your control. In this case, you must trust that the changes occurring are for your ultimate good. You may be experiencing something in your life that you do not want to happen but there is nothing you can do about it. Reassure yourself that, ultimately, all things, good or bad, happen for a reason, and in hindsight unwelcome events are often blessings in disguise.

storms

If a storm is a major part of your dream, try to link it to a situation in your life. Is there an argument brewing? Are your feelings of rage and anger about to burst? Your dream may be giving you information about your emotional state. Try to let out your feelings safely by talking about them to someone, or shouting them out on your own. Alternatively, face the problem head on with a constructive argument and try to clear the air. Remember, a storm is a short-lived burst of energy.

thunder and lightning

Thunder and lightning are dramatic events. They are often used in horror films to suggest a mood of dread and fear and to set the scene for something sinister to happen. But there is also a positive side to a violent storm: the air is cleared afterwards, and it is often followed by a sky of serene tranquillity.

In ancient times, thunder was thought to be the voice of an angry god. Have you upset or angered anyone? Or are you angry with anyone yourself?

Lightning is a sudden flash of light. In a dream this can signify inspiration. Have you been mulling over a problem that you can't solve? The lightning in your dream may be suggesting that the answer will reveal itself to you shortly.

rain

Rain in a dream will be linked to your emotions in some way. Rain is symbolic of tears; are yours tears of joy or grief? Is there a situation in your life that is making you miserable? Perhaps something is making you feel deliriously happy. Crying is a wonderful release of pent-up energy and can be soothing and cleansing, just as gentle rain.

snow

The first sight of virgin snow on the ground in winter is an exciting and wonderful experience. In a dream, the vision of a clean, untouched white landscape may be telling you that your life ahead is clear and blank, and you can make a fresh new start. But snow is also cold, and in a dream may signify a frosty atmosphere in one of your relationships.

ice

Water symbolises emotions, so if you dream about ice, consider whether your emotions are frozen and it would be helpful if you thawed them out. Your dream may also be suggesting that you should actually put something on ice, for example putting a forthcoming event on hold for a while. Are you walking on thin ice? This may imply that a certain situation could be very delicate. If the ice in your dream is melting, this could be an omen of a much gentler and warmer period ahead.

sunshine

The sun represents warmth, success, truth, light and abundance. The sun appearing in a cloudy sky suggests the end of a difficult period and the beginning of a much more positive time of joy and success. On the other hand, if the sun is setting and the light is fading, consider whether in your waking life you are being left in the dark over a certain situation. The sun is also a planet of fire; is your dream warning you away from someone or some situation that could be dangerous if you get too close?

mist and clouds

Both mist and clouds hinder vision. Look at your waking life and consider where such 'smoke screens' may be apparent. What is it in your life that you can't see clearly? Who or what is making your way ahead difficult and awkward? Is someone trying to confuse you?

nature

A whole range of dream themes come under this heading, including anything you might expect to find in a David Attenborough programme!

trees

Trees purify our air and have been seen mythologically as magical beings and the guardians of our planet. Throughout history they have provided us with us with food, medical ingredients and material for building shelter.

The tree of life represents strength, growth, wisdom and support. The roots of a tree symbolise your unconscious inner knowledge and your 'grip on life'. The trunk, being solid, represents your identity, personal strength and standing in life. It can also represent your family and other areas in your life that give you support. The branches are like those of a family tree; they represent your extended family, friends and acquaintances.

If you dream of a tree, notice what species it is, as different species of trees have different significance. These are the associations of some of the more common trees.

- **Oak:** Strength, power, support and honour

- **Willow:** Flexibility, femininity and motherhood (the weeping willow)

- **Rowan:** Protection and support. Plant this tree in the east of your garden and it will protect you from harm.

- **Bay:** The tree of success and prosperity. Planted at the north of the house, bay will protect against evil forces. Notice how many businesses and restaurants have two potted bay trees outside their main entrance. According to ancient wisdom (whether they know it or not), they are using the power of the bay to bring them success and to keep out unwanted guests. The Romans made crowns out of bay for their emperors, again as a symbol of success. Try planting a bay tree outside your front door – who knows what magic may happen.

A tree in your dream will certainly be bringing you a message. Notice whether the tree is healthy and strong. Is it in full bloom and bearing fruit? If so, this is a positive sign of plans coming to fruition. If the tree looks unhealthy, your dream may be telling you that you are not nurturing or looking after yourself properly. Trees blown over and with their roots showing may signify the end of one phase and the beginning of something new in your life. If the tree is shedding its leaves, the message could be that it's time to let go and leave something behind, in the knowledge that the tree will bear fruit and provide you with a better life.

plants

Since human life began we have used plants to heal and nourish us, but plants also have magical and spiritual properties. In our age of technological development the use of plant magic has dwindled, and at one point it looked as if it was in grave danger of being disregarded and forgotten. At last, interest in the properties of plants has begun to be rekindled, and some of the ancient wisdom that lies within us has been reawakened.

Let's have a look at some of the more common dream images of plants and flowers.

- **Grass:** Does the grass in your dream appear green and fertile? If so, this is a sign that you have a productive and creative time ahead of you. If the grass is too long, consider what in your life needs to be cut back or rationed. Are you lying in the grass and enjoying the experience of being at one with nature? If so, ask yourself whether you are in need of a rest or a holiday. If the grass is dry and parched, consider what or who you may be neglecting.

- **Nettles:** Nettles can give you a nasty sting. Who or what is getting on your nerves or under your skin?

- **Bouquets of flowers:** Flowers are sent as a sign of love and caring and also to let someone know you are thinking of them. Consider whether someone in your life is in need of your support and good wishes. A bouquet of flowers given to you in a dream could signify a cause for celebration and success to come.

⟨⟨ **Wild flowers:** A meadow full of wild flowers suggests ongoing pleasure and contentment in your life, without any restrictions. If, however, the flowers have grown out of control, consider what in your life has done the same.

If a particular flower features in your dream, try to work out what it means to you. For example, buttercups and daisies might remind you of your carefree childhood. A rose could represent love, but bear in mind that roses also have very nasty thorns!

animals

All animals have their own characteristics and traits. Native Americans have always been aware of the powers and magical qualities of animals, and we can all make use of this ancient wisdom to discover the inner meaning of animals in our dreams.

In your waking life you may be surrounded by domestic animals, such as cats, dogs, rabbits, fish, gerbils and birds, and these will often appear in your dreams. It is also very common for wild animals to make an appearance in dreams. In general, animal dreams may be making you aware of your own animal nature and sexuality; however, you should also consider the animal's particular traits, as a dream animal may be drawing your attention to its qualities, with the aim that you incorporate them into your life.

Think about the animal carefully, bring to mind your own feelings about it and consider its unique magical powers. Remember that whatever you read in this book, your personal view of the animal in your dream is the most relevant one when it comes to interpretation. It's no use generalising that mice are timid, furry and cuddly, if you yourself are actually terrified of them. Ask yourself whether in your life you are behaving in the same way as your dream animal – or would the animal's characteristics be able to help you if you did? If the animal's behaviour is negative, does this relate to the way you are behaving or to the way someone else in your life is? How can your dream animal be helpful to you in your current life situation?

Wild animals can symbolise the wild part of your own nature – the untamed passion and drive that lies deep within you. In the famous story 'The Strange Case of Dr Jekyll and Mr Hyde' by Robert Louis Stephenson, Dr Jekyll is a trustworthy, well-mannered gentleman by day, but at night he turns into Mr Hyde, who behaves like a wild beast. Mr Hyde symbolises the concealed wildness within us all.

Of course, there's an appropriate time and place to let your wild beast out. In any society it's important to play by the rules and conform, to obey the laws of the land and be respectful and considerate to our fellow human beings. This ensures your and everyone else's safety. However, our wild side is often unhealthily suppressed. One way to express your wildness is by channelling it into the creative arts, such as music and painting. Another way to let out this wild raw energy is through physical activities such as dancing or competitive sports.

The possible significance of some of the most commonly occurring dream animals is given below.

🦘 **Cats:** Cats are mysterious animals. Although they share our daily lives with us, they certainly have a mind of their own and you never quite know what they are thinking. Cats throughout the ages have been symbols of magic and mystery, and have been linked to witchcraft and the occult from the beginning of time. They represent the deep mysterious power associated with the feminine side of our nature, which is instinctive and intuitive. Cats are creatures of the night and the unknown. If a cat appears in your dream the message could be to trust your instinct, or to be crafty and sly in order to get something you desire.

🦘 **Dogs:** Where cats represent the female energy, dogs represent the masculine part of our nature. (Be aware that when I talk about male and female energies in this book, I am referring to the type of energy itself and not to men or women; as individuals we all have masculine and feminine energies within our personality.) Dogs are great companions – 'man's best friend'. They protect us and show us undying loyalty. Does the dog in your dream represent these qualities? Can you relate them to someone in your life? Dogs also bark to warn us of intruders. If the dog in your dream is barking, consider that this may be a specific warning dream. The warning could also be more general, suggesting that you should tread warily and not blindly trust those around you. Dogs can be frightening and vicious and may attack others in order to protect their owner. Is the dog in your dream protecting you or attacking you? Where in your life do you need protection? Should you be standing up for yourself more or are you rolling over in submission?

Dogs are pack animals and have a strong social structure. A dream of a pack of dogs could be drawing your attention to a group or gang of people.

Elephants: When these gentle beasts appear in your dream, the message is generally very positive. Elephants are the largest of all the animals and represent loyalty and strength; it is also said that 'an elephant never forgets'. A charging elephant in your dream could represent bitter anger against someone you once loved and cared for and who has let you down badly.

Foxes: Foxes are stunningly beautiful creatures that have a dreadful reputation and are often hunted and victimised. However, they are also devious and crafty in scavenging for food, and because of this are sometimes their own worst enemy. A fox in your dream may be suggesting that you should be crafty and observant in order to get what you want in a certain situation. On the other hand, it may be warning you that someone is deceiving you and that you should not trust this person.

Rachel's dream: *In my dream, my boyfriend is really a fox. While he's walking back home, after we've finished snogging outside my house, he turns into a fox and comes back to look for me. He's snooping around outside my house all night.*

〽 **Interpretation:** It was very clear that Rachel did not totally trust her boyfriend. I wondered what she thought he was after. It didn't take Rachel long to work out that her boyfriend was not content with just a snog; he had a bit more in mind than that. Her dream was warning her of this.

〽 **Resolution:** Rachel became aware that her boyfriend might use sly tactics to get what he wanted. She responded by being more careful with him. She let him know right away that a snog was all he was going to get!

〽 **Horses:** In their natural environment horses are wild, powerful, swiftly moving animals. Throughout history we have developed an amazing rapport with this magnificent animal in many areas of our lives. They have also been used as beasts of burden, in farming, for transport, to carry messages, as cavalry in war and more recently for sporting activities and pleasure. Horses have always been symbolically linked with nobility and wealth, and to dream of horses can therefore be a good omen for the future. Likewise, horseshoes have always represented good luck. When a horse appears in your dream consider the context carefully. Is the horse wild or tame? Are you riding it in a controlled fashion or is it bolting, taking you with it? How does this relate to your waking life? Are you in control of a precarious situation, or do you feel as if something in your life is running away with you? If the horse is running wild and free with the wind, this may suggest that you should trust your own wild inner nature and break free from the shackles of conformity. Horses are also a symbol of male sexuality and prowess – we sometimes refer to a man who is very sexually active as a stud. If you are a man, this type of dream may be putting you in touch with your own sexual power. It is said that women dream more often about horses than men do, perhaps because the wildness and unrestraint of this male-associated image is sexually arousing.

Lions: Lions are one of the most feared and respected of animals. In dreams they often represent strength, power and a masculine energy. Ask yourself where in your waking life these qualities are called for. Does the lion represent you, or is it someone in authority? If the lion is caged, ask yourself if you have feelings that you want to keep safely locked away, or, alternatively, that you would like to express freely but are afraid to because you are scared of your own power. If you are fighting or taming the lion in your dream, consider what situation or person this may relate to in your waking life and how you can use the qualities that the lion represents to help you in your battle. Consider whether you are acting in a rather cowardly way about something in your waking life. Does the lion signify that you need to find your strength, power and courage?

Rabbits: Rabbits are often family pets and are generally thought of as cuddly, fluffy loveable creatures. Do you have an admirer who sees you in this way? Is somebody falling helplessly in love with you? In the wild rabbits are prolific breeders. Is the dream suggesting that you should restrict your sexual behaviour?

Rats: Rats are classed as vermin and as such are considered dirty and unhygienic. They have been the carriers of some of the world's most deadly diseases, including the plague. They are looked upon as sly and untrustworthy. If a rat appears in your dream, ask yourself whether there is someone around you who you do not trust and who could do you harm? On the other hand, Michael Jackson's song 'Ben' is about a rat he loves and thinks of as his only friend. In Chinese astrology the rat is a kind, gentle, social creature. Always bear in mind that your own personal view is very significant in how you interpret your dream.

Snakes: Many people have a phobia about snakes. This is not surprising, since many species of snake inflict poisonous bites that can be deadly. Other species can crush a human body by wrapping themselves around it and constricting their muscles. Snakes like to hide in the dark, and have the ability to shed their skins, so renewing themselves. No wonder the snake is hugely feared and held in awe. Throughout history, the snake has been used to symbolise many qualities. Adam and Eve were tempted by a serpent, which has been seen as representing evil and the devil. Snakes can sometimes symbolise slyness, cunning and deception. Ask yourself whether someone in your life is being a 'snake in the grass' – untrustworthy and menacing. In many Eastern traditions, the snake is a symbol of knowledge, feminine intuition and wisdom. It also symbolises kundalini – an energetic force within the human body. Snakes also have sexual connotations and are considered to be phallic symbols.

Tigers: Tigers are stunningly beautiful creatures – a truly awesome sight. They symbolise the powerful, magnetic and seductive feminine side of our nature. A tiger appearing in your dreams could suggest a need to utilise all the stunning magnificence in yourself to face a certain situation and achieve what you want. Tigers can also be a symbol of ferocious love and loyalty.

Cows: Cows are large gentle beasts that have lived close to us for much of our history, providing us with milk and meat. They often symbolise motherhood and the maternal, so if a cow shows up in your dreams, consider whether mothering is an issue in your waking life. They also represent wealth and prosperity, for they not only sustain life but were also once considered to be a measure of a person's wealth. To Hindus cows are holy animals. In India they are allowed to roam freely throughout the towns, where they are fed and cared for by everyone and never killed for meat.

Ducks and hens: Because they are domesticated egg-layers, these birds are particularly associated with eggs. If you dream about ducks or hens, ask yourself whether your dream is sending you a message about fertility and sexuality? Are you, or is someone close to you, thinking about having a baby? In pagan rituals eggs often symbolise the dawn of a new life.

Goats: Goats are hardy animals and can survive in the hardest of climates; they also eat anything. A goat in your dreams may be sending you a message about your ability to endure through a certain difficult situation.

Sheep and rams: Sheep may denote a life of comfort and ease but one that is also without drive or ambition. Ask yourself whether life is feeling like this for you. Have you lost your individuality and zest? Consider how this dream can help you: it may be a message of contentment but it may also be the opposite. Rams are aggressive and sexually rampant. Does this ring with your own behaviour at times? Or does someone else in your waking life behave in this way?

Pigs: Although the pig is such a lovely animal, sadly, to dream of one is not favourable. Pigs usually represent greed, obesity and laziness. You call someone a pig if they are mean and unkind to you, and 'pig' is also a term of insult for the police. But remember that you must always look at animals in dreams in the context of your own feeling towards the particular type of animal in order to make an accurate interpretation.

Frogs and toads: Frogs and toads have been associated with magic and witchcraft since ancient times. In 'The Frog Prince', a well-known childhood fable, the princess kisses an ugly frog and it turns into a handsome prince. What or who in your life might you give the benefit of the doubt to? Are you thinking badly of someone who doesn't deserve it? Frogs and toads are also symbols of sexuality due to the large amount of spawn that they produce each year and the sperm-like tadpoles that it becomes.

Fish: A dream involving fish may be a mirror of your emotional state. Do you feel like a fish out of water? Do you feel as if you have 'gone in too deep' in a certain situation? The fish is also a phallic symbol and represents the sperm on its journey to fertilise the female ovum. Since the earliest times the fish has been a symbol of Christianity, and many of the parables of Jesus are about fish and fishermen, so if you dream of fish it's possible that you need to look deeper into your religious beliefs. If you dream about a specific fish, consider its particular characteristics. For example, sharks are dangerous; pike lurk in deep, dark muddy waters and can be threatening; and some tropical fish are exotic, beautiful and graceful. What are the qualities of the fish in your dream? How do they relate to your waking life? How could they be helpful to you?

If you dream that you are fishing, ask yourself what you're fishing for. Is your dream trying to tell you that you need to find out more information about something in your life?

Ami's dream: *I had the dream that I was eaten alive by a shark. It was horrible. When I woke up I couldn't work out what this dream meant.*

Interpretation: Ami told me that she was being bullied at school and the situation had become pretty bad. We worked out that the shark in her dream represented the bully who was giving her a hard time.

Resolution: The purpose of the nightmare was to get Ami to do something about the bullying. She decided to discuss the nightmare with her mum and then found that she was also able to tell her about being bullied. Her mum dealt with the situation by going to see the headmistress at Ami's school.

Crabs: The crab is a homely creature that is protected by a hard shell. A dream about a crab could be a message about your own protection, or it could indicate that someone around you has a hard exterior and a soft inside. Crabs have huge pincers that can give you a nasty bite. Is your dream a warning not to get too close to someone who could do the same?

insects and creepy-crawlies

It can be very frightening to come across creepie-crawlies in everyday life, but it's even worse when they turn up giant-sized and extra ferocious in your dream world! If you dream about insects, ask yourself whether something or someone is 'bugging' you? Who or what is getting on your nerves or making your skin crawl? Make a note of the kind of insect you are dreaming about and consider its characteristics. Where and how do they show up in your life?

Biting and stinging insects: Insects and bugs are small creatures, but they can often bite back. If you dream of biting insects, such as fleas or mosquitoes, ask yourself whether someone in your waking life is trying to attack or get their own back on you. If you dream about wasps, bees or other stinging insects, ask yourself if there is a situation in your life where you might 'get stung' or come to harm? Is a certain person in your life behaving in a suspicious way? Might they turn nasty on you? I once had a dream in which I was badly stung by wasps while I was talking to my next-door neighbour. Within the next few weeks my neighbour issued a court summons over a boundary dispute. The dream was an astoundingly accurate warning. I was well and truly stung!

Tom's dream: *I am walking down this long country road. As I walk, I crush lots of creepy-crawly insects. I can hear them crunching under my football boots. I don't even look down; I just keep on walking, because I have to get to the end of the road.*

Interpretation: Tom is a talented and determined football player. His family had moved house and he was finding it difficult to get to football games, as his team was now a long way away. It seemed as if there was always something getting in the way. These small obstacles are symbolised in his dream by the creepy-crawlies. However, Tom just walks over them and keeps on walking; he knows he's got to 'get there' regardless of any obstacles.

🌙 **Resolution:** Tom explained to his parents how important it was for him to get to his football matches. They asked around, and he now gets a lift to games each week from one of the other team members' parents.

extinct and mythological creatures

This category is pretty large and can include just about any fabulous monster you have read about in an ancient myth or seen in a schlock horror movie. To get you thinking, the following are possible symbolic meanings of just a few of the creatures you may discover in your dreams.

🌙 **Dinosaurs:** Dinosaurs are, of course, extinct, so if you dream about them, ask yourself who or what is past its sell-by date. Has a relationship run its course? Is there a part of your life that needs changing or replacing with a newer improved version?

🌙 **Dragons:** The dragon, known for its fiery breath and ferocious nature, has featured in myths since ancient times. St George reputedly slaughtered a dragon and saved the English nation. His banner represented the English team in 2002's World Cup football matches; symbolically this image gave the message that the team would fight bravely till the end and come away victorious. England didn't win the World Cup, but at least they had the right intention! A dragon in your dreams symbolises a fierce tenacious attitude. Is this one that you need somewhere in your waking life? Do you feel as if your life is a battle? If so, what or who are you fighting? Is the dragon something you need to slay, or could it show you the way forward? Perhaps you can use the qualities of the dragon to achieve your goal. The dragon also guards treasure. Are you fiercely protecting a person or a situation you value?

- **Vampires:** Vampires represent the dark side of our character – the part we prefer to keep hidden. Vampires, of course, feed off the blood of a living soul. Ask yourself whether a person or situation in your life is sapping your strength and energy? Is someone using you? Are you being bullied – or are you bullying someone else?

- **Werewolves:** Werewolves often represent the shadow part of us. If you dream about a werewolf, it may indicate that there is something hidden in your shadow side that you need to bring to light. This may be buried anger or it may be some aspect of yourself that you find disgusting and shameful. Alternatively, has someone in your life shown a side to their character that you find disgusting? Try to work out why this beast has ventured into your dream world. Is another person making you feel this way? Let me emphasise that we all have dark sides to our personality, and these can be positive if expressed in a way that is safe. If your dark thoughts disturb you, try expressing them by writing or drawing to bring them out of the deep recesses of your mind.

life concepts

In this grouping I have included anything that affects your daily life, from huge events such as birth and death to the more mundane issues of what we like to eat and how we live our lives – in the public eye or out of it.

birth

A dream of a birth can be a wish fulfilment dream on a very literal level: if you've been trying for a baby, it may be telling you that you are pregnant. However, in the majority of cases the meaning of this dream is likely to be more metaphorical. The dream birth could signify the beginning of a new phase in your life or symbolise a new project, which you may think of as 'your baby'.

A birth represents new life, fresh impetus, changing horizons, the letting-go of something old and the creation of something new. This could be a new relationship (with a lover or friend), a new job or venture, or perhaps a new home. It could even be a shift in attitude towards a religion or belief system.

If pregnancy rather than birth is the theme of your dream, this suggests that something new is likely to develop, but not immediately.

A dream of a birth in which the baby is still-born can be distressing but should not be taken literally. Essentially, the message here is that something which you are hoping for is likely to fall short of your expectations.

death

Dreaming of a death or a birth nearly always triggers a strong response and will often form a firm imprint within your mind. These occasions are such vivid moments in the physical world that of course they are almost always powerful images in the dream world. A death, like a birth, calls for a celebration of someone's life, but unlike a birth, which is usually a time of great joy, death entails inevitable feelings of grief and loss. Both deaths and births make us aware of our own mortality.

All of us without exception will die, and this truth is frightening us all. However, a death in a dream is unlikely to mean that you or anyone else is going to die any time soon. Symbolically, dream deaths can have many meanings, but the most obvious is that a phase or situation in your life is over or is shortly to come to an end. Remember, the bright side to every ending is the dawn of a new beginning.

There are many situations in life that can be symbolised by death: the end of a relationship, a change of career path, a change of heart – in fact, any situation in which you are confronted by change and from which you are moving on. It is important to say goodbye to what is old and leaving our world, and also to find value in what is now gone, even if the memory is painful. Let it pass and then move forwards towards your future.

If you keep having dreams about death or dying, think about your current situation. Is there something in your life that you are clinging on to? This dream could be urging you to move on in your life. Are you resisting? The future is the big unknown, and sometimes we feel safer holding on to what we are familiar with. If this is the case, then try to let go and make space for the new.

〽 **Barbara's dream:** *In my dream I am ill and dying. I'm lying in my parents' bed and people are coming to visit me and say goodbye. I know that this will be the last time I see my family and friends. I don't feel worried at all, even though I know I'm going to die. The sun is shining and it's a nice day. But I feel very different when I wake up; the dream really shook me up – it felt so real.*

〽 **Interpretation:** This was a significant dream for Barbara. It preyed on her mind because it seemed to portray her death, but at the same time in the actual dream there was a complete absence of anxiety. When I talked to Barbara she told me that she had recently made a new commitment in her television career. As we discussed this new development, it emerged that her dream was an acknowledgement that she was in the process of saying goodbye to her old life.

〽 **Resolution:** Once Barbara understood that her dream was not really about death but about the beginning of an exciting new phase in her life, she was able to relax and come to terms with it.

being chased

An overwhelming fear is usually present when you are being chased. Often, you do not know what is behind you. You simply run as fast as you can to escape the clutches of the mystery attacker. Sometimes this thing actually catches you, but more often than not you wake up before it gets you.

The way to address this kind of dream is to deduce who or what is chasing you. The attacker is sometimes an aspect of yourself that you are ignoring. You might find it useful here to look back at the section on monsters (see page 45). On the other hand, there may be an issue that you're forever putting off. Maybe you regularly think about it but keep telling yourself you'll do it later. Whatever this issue is, it's urgent enough for your subconscious to get anxious about it, because it's plaguing you in your dreams, chasing you and desperately trying to get your attention. This type of dream is likely to continue indefinitely, with greater frequency and urgency, until you finally do something about it!

falling

This dream event is often a challenge to place your trust in life. Are you a control freak? Do you become anxious when you're not in complete command? Are you battling against all the odds to control a situation that is really beyond your control? Are you afraid of letting someone go or of allowing them to make their own decisions in life? Maybe love is troubling you, as this isn't something you can control.

It may be that you are on the crest of a major life change and your dream is highlighting your inner fears and insecurities about the unknown future ahead. If this is the case, talk to a loved one and ask for reassurance. Talking about your fears usually helps you to sleep better.

🜲 **Jo's dream:** *I'm walking with my family up a hill. When we get to the top I fall off the edge of a cliff. I wake up before I hit the bottom.*

🜲 **Interpretation:** Jo was leaving home to go to university in London. The hill represented her consistent achievement in life. Throughout her life, her family had always supported her every step of the way. Her fall from the cliff edge highlighted her fear of stepping out into the world alone. Her anxiety was understandable and is common among young people moving away from home for the first time.

🜲

Dream Themes

Resolution: Jo let her parents know about her concerns. They told her that of course she would continue to have their support after she had left home. This was just the reassurance she needed.

anxiety dreams

Dreams accompanied by feelings of fear, insecurity, or panic are classed as nightmares. You will find a section on Nightmares starting on page 41.

toilet dreams

This a type of dream that you may tend not to discuss with anyone, because toilet dreams can be embarrassing and humiliating. They are, however, very common.

Are you desperately searching for a toilet but cannot find one? Sometimes this dream is a very simple message from your subconscious that you do indeed need to go. With any luck you'll wake up and get to the toilet in time. If you do have a problem with bed-wetting, talk to your doctor. Bed-wetting can be a medical problem or it may have a psychological cause. In either case there are effective treatments and therapies.

If you don't need to go to the toilet, you may be holding on to something in a way that is not good for you. This could be a situation or an emotion. Are you in need of an emotional discharge about something? If so, when you deal with it, you will feel an immense release!

Suzie's dream: *In my dream I want to go to the toilet and I do a number two right in the middle of the road. The road is old and dusty and there are no cars. There are lots of people walking by and they are looking at me, but nobody pays any real attention.*

Interpretation: Suzie had a summer job, which she hated. She felt that she was being taken advantage of just because she was a student. In her dream she was letting go of her anger in public, and she didn't care who knew about it.

꧁ **Resolution:** Suzie went into work, told her employers what she thought about them and quit her job. She gave herself the problem of finding another job, but, on the other hand, this assertive action made her feel good about herself.

Sex

Interestingly, girls dream about sex as often as boys do, but the type of dream differs. Boys tend to dream about women who are totally uninhibited and up for anything. Girls on the other hand tend to dream about guys who are knowledgeable and virile but accommodate their desires.

Sexual dreams can be exciting, erotic and carefree, and may involve events that are unlikely to happen in waking life, such as having sex in public. They may express thoughts that you forbid yourself from indulging in in your waking life. If this is the case, your dream may be suggesting that you try to take sex less seriously as an issue. Sex may appear in your dreams as wish fulfilment, especially if you are feeling sexually frustrated. Such dreams can often leave you feeling – unnecessarily – guilty and ashamed.

Dreaming that you are having sex with someone of the same sex does not necessarily mean that you are gay, although it may signify that you are assessing that part of your personality that has erotic responses to people of your own sex, and on some level we all do. On the other hand it may mean that you need to celebrate your femininity or masculinity.

Dreams of being raped can be profoundly disturbing. Ask yourself whether there is someone in your life who is taking advantage of you, or who makes you feel threatened and vulnerable.

If you have frequent sexual dreams, consider how comfortable or uncomfortable you are with the whole issue of sex. It's very normal and natural to feel a little embarrassed about the subject, especially if you're at the point in your life where you're discovering what it's all about. Thinking about sex is the most natural thing on earth. Nevertheless, it may be hard to talk to your parents about sex – and they may also find it difficult to talk about sex with you. If you need someone to discuss sexual issues with and you can't think of anyone suitable among your family and friends, try asking your doctor to refer you to a counsellor. He or she will be able to listen to you with an open mind and without getting embarrassed.

body image

Body image is a major factor in most of our lives and is especially delicate when you are growing up and developing your character. During our younger years we all feel the need to conform, to be accepted by our friends and to blend in. This is evident in the clothes we wear, our tastes in music, our hairstyle and so on. There's nothing worse than your parents buying you clothes that are functional and good quality but look absolutely naff. Having the right image and fitting in with your mates is really important when you're a teenager.

As you start to mature, however, all this begins to change, and you may find that you no longer want to conform with everyone else. You start to formulate your own ideas, and you may agree to differ with the general consensus of opinion. You begin to make choices and decisions based on your own volition. This stage marks your development as an individual. You are discovering your true identity.

Everybody wants to feel good about themselves, and everybody wants to be accepted in society as an equal, no matter what their image is. Feelings of insecurity and uncertainty about the way that others perceive you can be a constant source of worry. Fashion, music, and similar trends are always changing, and so the pressure to keep your image up-to-date is considerable.

You will, I am sure, be familiar with your own personal critic who resides permanently inside your head. You could think of it as a little gremlin that chats away to you, sometimes non-stop, from inside. Here are a few examples:

- **Girls:** You look too fat in that; your hair is the wrong colour; everyone will laugh at you if your wear that; your boobs are too small; your bum is too big.

- **Boys:** You're too small; you've got no muscles; she'll never fancy you; you're such a geek; everyone will think you're soft.

Which of these self-criticisms crops up often for you? How many more can you think of? These incessant insecurities will certainly manifest themselves in your dream world.

hair

In one well-known bible story, Samson is said to be the strongest man alive. However, when Delilah cuts off his long, thick hair, his fabulous strength immediately deserts him. Hair has always been a symbol for strength and vitality. It is also an obvious outward sign of beauty, and healthy glowing hair can inspire you with self-confidence. You can imagine how difficult it must be to lose your hair prematurely, either because nature decrees or through illness or as a side-effect of medication. If you dream that something has happened to your hair, ask yourself whether somewhere in your life you feel weak and devitalised. Who or what might be making you feel this way?

- **Lizzy's dream:** *In my dream, my hair turns into bubblegum and all my friends are trying to bite a bit off it.*

- **Interpretation and resolution:** Lizzy had been chosen from hundreds of pupils to perform at the Queen's Golden Jubilee concert in London. She was feeling really good about herself and was the envy of all her friends. Her dream reflected this: her friends admired her so much they all wanted a piece of whatever it was that she had. The dream was warning Lizzy to enjoy the occasion without letting her success go to her head.

- **Resolution:** Lizzy was determined to make the most of the concert without getting big-headed about being chosen.

eyebrows

Human eyebrows don't appear to have any function at all, other than to frame and create expression within the face; however, if we examine our distant relations, the apes and monkeys, we can see that eyebrows originated as an important form of protection for the vulnerable eyes. In many animals the eyebrows are very bushy and brightly coloured. When the animal frowns, they give the impression that it's bigger and fiercer than it really is; thus they deter predators.

Dreaming that your eyebrows have vanished can represent feelings of insecurity and vulnerability. Just think for a moment about how you would feel if you had no eyebrows – a little bit exposed I imagine.

Lynne's dream: *In my dream I go to school and everyone is looking at me because I have no eyebrows.*

Interpretation: Lynne had just been made a school prefect. She was a bit unsure about how she would cope with her friends now that she had been given a position of authority. The dream was highlighting her feeling of vulnerability.

Resolution: Once she was aware of her conflicting feelings, Lynne was able to give herself time to think about how she would negotiate being in a position of authority and being a friend at the same time. The situation still felt challenging but no longer seemed so threatening.

clothes

Your clothes are an expression and extension of your personality. By the way you dress you can give very clear messages to others about who you are. Some of the many styles of dress that are easy to read include:

- Trendy designer
- Casual and laid back
- Grungy and scruffy
- Sporty
- Gothic
- Old-fashioned
- Cheap and tacky
- Sexy
- Punk
- Leathers, biker
- Fancy dress
- Science fiction

If you or someone else in your dream is dressed in one of these ways, what statement might they be making? Are they wearing old-fashioned Victorian clothing, such as long dresses with tightly corseted waists and suits with high stuffy collars? The message here could relate to your attitude – or someone else's – which may be out-dated and restrictive. Sexy leather clothing could be prompting you to spice up your life and get in touch with your sexuality. Sci-fi gear could be suggesting that your outlook is way ahead of its time, and the grunge look that you chill out a bit more – or, alternatively, smarten up.

footwear

Shoes represent movement and advancement in life, and a dream of a new pair of shoes suggests success. Did you dream about a new pair of Nike trainers? They could represent an exciting new project, full of life and vitality. Alternatively, they could be a more direct message from your subconscious mind: get some exercise!

celebrities

We have become a nation obsessed with celebrities and their life styles. The days of the elusive film star shielded from publicity in their reclusive mountain hideaway are no more; a celebrity's life is now a public one, and the new phenomenon of 'reality' TV programmes such as *Big Brother* and *Pop Idol* makes ordinary people celebrities overnight.

Public and media opinion combined have an extraordinary amount of power and influence over celebrities and can make or break them – as in the splitting up of pop group Hearsay. Glossy magazines, tabloids, chat shows, internet sites ... the media relentlessly broadcast the latest celebrity gossip: what they're wearing, which parties they've been to, who they're sleeping with now, who they've slept with in the past and what they eat for breakfast. And we're all gagging to hear the latest. A celebrity has to present the image that the public wants if they're to remain in the limelight.

If a celebrity appears in one of your dreams, remember that everyone and everything you dream about is telling you something about yourself. Take a look at the celebrity and answer the following questions.

⟩ What do you like about them and why?

⟩ What do you dislike about them and why?

⟩ What in your answers is describing a part of yourself?

⟩ What in your answers would you like to be describing a part of yourself?

Let's say, for example, that in your dream you're getting married and having a big church wedding. You're walking down the aisle smiling at your guests. You reach the front of the church and turn around to face the bridegroom ... only to discover that he's your favourite pop star. Sadly, your dream is unlikely to mean that you're going to marry him. Your dream bridegroom is more likely to represent qualities that you are looking for in yourself or a partner. If, for instance, the groom in your dreams is someone known for his kindness, ask yourself whether kindness is a quality that you possess or one that you lack and need to cultivate. On the other hand, is kindness something that you require in a partner?

Another example: let's say you dream you're in bed with Kylie Minogue. It's very likely that this dream is about sexual image and desire. If you're a girl, you may have a deep wish to portray the same image as Kylie. The dream could be suggesting you try to emulate some of her qualities in order to project yourself in a more sensual way. If you're a guy, this dream is almost certainly sexual in nature and needs little explanation!

Sonya's dream: *In real life I'm frightened of lifts so I always take the stairs, but in my dream I walk into a lift – and find myself standing next to David Beckham. It breaks down and we're trapped. In the dream I'm not frightened of being in a lift at all – surprise, surprise!*

Interpretation: Well, lucky you, Sonya. What a wonderful dream. Sadly though, it's unlikely to be predictive – although it does hold a considerable amount of interesting information. Firstly, let's look at David Beckham, his characteristics and qualities:

- He's an exceptionally *talented* football player.
- He's the youngest captain ever of the England football team.
- He's a natural born *leader*.
- He's a stunningly *attractive* man.
- He's a fashion icon and *trend-setter*.
- He's happily married to another trendy celebrity, Posh Spice.
- He's a *family* man.
- He's made the big time on *talent* alone.
- He does have a funny way of speaking!

Sonya, needed to look at these qualities and achievements and decide which were relevant to her own life. Were they qualities she would like to possess herself, or qualities she desired in a partner?

In this dream, Sonya does something she wouldn't normally do: entering the lift. The outcome, however, is very favourable. This dream could be urging her to go beyond her normal limits – perhaps the results will be equally positive.

 **Resolution:** In the list of David Beckham's qualities, Sandra found that she had a lot of information to ponder, and she decided to spend some time doing this. She also determined to get over her lift phobia – and in fact this proved easier than she expected.

food

Eating is a major part of our daily lives. Not only is it a necessity for sustaining life but it is also one of life's great pleasures. A meal can be a celebration feast, a casual picnic, a romantic dinner for two or a microwave quick-fix for couch potatoes.

Consider the context in which food appears in your dream. If there is a feast before your eyes this may be symbolic of your success – a meal to honour your achievements. If you dream of a family meal, what is the atmosphere around the table and how are you feeling? Is the food appetising and nourishing or is it rotten and unpalatable? If the latter, consider whether your waking life is nourishing you enough.

Does the food in your dream look great but taste bitter and foul? Ask yourself what in your life looks good on the outside but is rotten inside. Alternatively, this dream could be a message of self-denial. Ask yourself whether or not you deserve the best that life has to offer. If the dream cupboard or fridge is bare, ask yourself whether you desire something so badly in your waking life that it resembles hunger pains. Is it love, acknowledgement, understanding, support? Gorging on food in your dream could also have the same meaning.

If food is a constant focal point in your dreams consider the possibility that you have an eating disorder. If you feel this could be the case, please seek help. Eating problems are very common in the teenage years and relate to personal issues that have not been addressed properly. Your doctor will be able to refer you to a counsellor.

fruit

Fruit represents fertility and sexuality and has traditionally been a symbol of immortality. When ripe, fruit is sensual and oozing with lush juices. It's easy to understand therefore why it represents the pleasures of the flesh. If you dream about fruit, consider what role pleasure and sensuality play – or don't play – in your waking life. The following fruits have certain specific connotations.

- **Apples:** The apple is a symbol of temptation.

- **Bananas:** The banana is wholesome and nutritious. A single banana is also a phallic symbol – it resembles the penis.

- **Figs:** The fig has always been a symbol of fertility; it is a fruit holding thousands of tiny seeds within it.

- **Grapes:** Wine is made from the juice of grapes and is a widespread source of pleasure and enjoyment. Grapes symbolise riches and prosperity, as well as sensuality and the pleasures of the flesh.

- **Peaches and melons:** When ripe, these fruits are juicy and delicious. They are often used to describe women's breasts.

drinks

The human body is mainly made up of water. Water is essential to life; we can survive for weeks without food but only days without water. The following drinks have particular significance.

-  **Tea and coffee:** Throughout most of the world a cup of tea or coffee is part of the social culture. The ritual of drinking tea and coffee marks a time of withdrawal from the busyness of the day – time to relax and gather your thoughts or chat with your friends in a relaxed way as you gather your energy for the next phase of the day. The tea/coffee break is a traditional part of the day. A dream about drinking tea or coffee can suggest that you should take some time out for yourself and not work incessantly.

- **Alcohol:** Alcohol is either the demon drink or a harmless social pleasure. In your dream which does it signify? The need to drink alcohol can represent a desire to escape, to be 'out of it'. If you aren't coping with some aspect of your life, consider why you feel the need to escape from it.

objects and activities

Now we look at material things – from your home to your dad's car – and activities such as sport and travel.

houses and buildings

Houses and homes represent stability within your life and also your current emotional state. Different areas of the house reflect different aspects of your life. For instance, the basement of a house represents your past and can refer to your childhood. It can also represent your deepest thoughts, which you share with no one but yourself. The living room relates to your present life, and attics foretell the future or portray your greatest wishes and desires. Doors are considered to represent the mouth and windows the eyes. If there is a problem with a door in your dream, consider whether there is something in your waking life that you have difficulty talking about. Can you see through the windows of your dream house? Are they suggesting that there is an issue in your life you need to look at or one that you do not see clearly?

previous homes

Dreaming about a house that you used to live in is common and is a means of accessing old feelings that you may have buried. How did you feel in your dream? Were the memories fond childhood ones or were they painful? How do they relate to your present situation? Are you going through a difficult time right now and looking back to the good old days? Is there a current problem that you could deal with better if you drew on experiences gained from dealing with a similar problem in the past? Are you visiting your old life to comfort yourself, or is your subconscious mind drawing your attention to the differences between your previous and current situations in order to highlight your progress?

cellars

These can be dark, damp and a bit spooky, and may contain difficult memories from childhood. What are you doing down in the cellar? If you're sifting through rubbish, what is it you need to remember? Is there something from childhood that you need to find out about – or is there something you need to leave behind? Have you discovered old lost treasures? How can they be helpful to you now? Are you locked in the cellar and frightened? Is your dream asking you to look at a weakness or a feeling from childhood that you have still not dealt with?

halls, passages and stairways

These are all spaces that link one room to another. Dreaming of these areas suggests changes ahead – they represent the transitional period between leaving one area or phase of your life and entering the next.

Staircases are often used in paintings and films to symbolise a rise or fall in someone's position in life. A dream of an ascending staircase or escalator can indicate a promotion of some sort or progress towards something better. Ascending stairs can also represent higher realms such as heaven – whereas descending stairs have historically represented a downward journey into hell. A more likely interpretation of a dream of a descending staircase, however, would be taking a step backwards, or a need to take time out for thought and reflection.

bedrooms and lounges

Bedrooms and lounges are places for relaxation and rest. Both rooms represent security and comfort. The bedroom, of course, also has sexual implications. In order to discover the meaning of these images in individual dreams, you need to assess the accompanying feelings.

If you dream of a bedroom containing a large and empty bed, ask yourself whether in real life you desire to start a relationship. If the bed is inviting and warm, consider whether you are in need of rest and sleep. Are you closing the curtains in your dream and then getting into bed? This suggests a need to be alone or to block out the world for a while. Are you opening curtains and getting up to a bright day? This could mean that you have rested or taken time out to assess something, and now you are fresh, strong and raring to go.

If you dream of a lounge, is it cosy and welcoming or cold and forbidding? Are there areas in your life that feel like the lounge in your dream?

bathrooms and showers

Bathrooms are luxurious and laid-back. If you dream of a bathroom, ask yourself whether you're in need of some quality time on your own. Are you long overdue for some pampering? Have you not been giving yourself enough attention? What do you need to prepare yourself for? Is there something in your life you need to cleanse yourself of?

Showers are invigorating and energising. They wake you up after a period of sleep and cleanse you after a workout at the gym. If you dream of a shower, ask yourself whether you have a sense of excitement and anticipation that something exhilarating is about to happen in your waking life? Are you filled with a 'go-getting' energy or is your dream suggesting that you should be?

toilets

Toilets are private places where you let go of your unwanted waste. If you dream of a toilet, ask yourself what in your life you need to let go of badly? Are you holding on to unwanted feelings or relationships that you know you would be better flushing away?

kitchens

The kitchen is often the social and focal point of the house, and it is, of course, the space in which food is prepared and cooked. What are you doing in the kitchen in your dream? Are you preparing something? Is there a new phase around the corner in your waking life that requires planning and preparation? What kind of meal are you preparing? Is it a meal for yourself or for several people? Dreams of cooking often signify a period of creativity. Innovations and successful projects, like great food, are the result of time and thoughtful preparation.

Take into account the type of food you're dealing with. Raw meat suggests a male energy and points to a plan that is ambitious and requires drive and determination – a project you can 'get your teeth into'. If you're preparing or eating a meal consisting of soft delicate ingredients, probably a female energy is required. Consider what area of your life is in need of nurturing and some gentle input. If the food is sweet, then you may be in a need of a treat. Are you going through a tough and stressful time in your life? Food can be used (or abused) as an emotional buffer. Are you someone who raids the biscuit barrel every time you feel down or despondent?

Ovens provide the analogy of baking, suggesting that a project needs time to reach a successful conclusion – so don't rush in too quickly and spoil it. Leaving things to simmer is a similar analogy, as is putting something 'on the back burner'.

If you're hungry in this kitchen, ask yourself what you're hungry for in your life.

new rooms

Entering a room in your dream that you do not recognise may signify that changes need to happen in your life – or are about to happen. Take a look at the room and absorb its features and characteristics. It could be giving you insight into the direction of your future. Is the room newly decorated – suggesting a complete change in your life – or is it tatty and out of date? If the latter, consider what in your waking life needs revitalising.

palaces and castles

Palaces and castles exist in real life and are also striking images from fairy tales and legends. If you dream of a palace or castle, ask yourself if you are discontented with your life. Do you feel that something better is waiting for you? Do you want a lifestyle of power and luxury? Are you waiting for someone to come and rescue you? Do you feel deep down inside that you are special and should be treated as such? Or is your life dull and boring, and do you wish to escape from it?

Consider the appearance and feel of the palace or castle. Is it high on a hill, unapproachable and cold? If so, does it remind you of a person in your life? Is it a symbol of protection or of prison? Do you need protection or do you feel like running away from something that is restricting you in some way?

games and sport

Games are social activities and are generally played for fun and pleasure. Sports demand skill and talent as well as a competitive nature if you are to succeed. Both are energising activities that are challenging and confidence-building.

Dreams about sporting activities and games relate to your sense of team spirit. They can also provide insight into how you deal with challenges and obstacles in your life. Is your dream trying to make you aware of the qualities you need to get to the top or how to play the game of life? Are you spectating or are you playing a game or sport? Is it a team sport such as football, or is it a self-motivated activity such as golf, running or chess? If you are not part of a team in your dream, consider whether you would like to be part of one in your waking life. Belonging to a team can fulfil a desire to be accepted and needed. On the other hand, is your dream suggesting that you lack team spirit and are perhaps too self-centred?

football

Football is a team game but it also contains strong individuals within it. If you're playing football in your dream, are you a defensive player or an attacking player? How is this relevant to your waking life? Are you happy being a squad player, or do you yearn to be the star of the show, the goal scorer? If you scored a goal in your dream, what did it feel like? If you missed a goal or penalty, what did this feel like? Is there a disappointment in your life that is continually making you feel like a failure?

playground games

A dream in which you are in the playground is generally taking you back in time for a reason. What are you feeling in your dream? Are the childhood memories pleasant ones – suggesting that you need to look at the good things in your life – or are they painful ones? If the latter, what current situation in your life is causing you to remember them?

card games

Card games involve mental skill and agility. This type of dream carries a message of caution, suggesting that you should think carefully about decisions in your life at the moment. Also, be aware of other people around you: someone may be trying to outsmart you and take advantage. Are you cheating in your dream? If so, are you cheating in a situation in real life?

contact sports

Sports such as wrestling, boxing and karate are activities that crucially involve an opponent. If you dream about this kind of sport, ask yourself who or what you are wrestling with in your waking life. Are you dealing with a difficult problem that is demanding all of your strength? What are you finding challenging? Do you feel as though you have to defend yourself? Who or what is getting the better of you? How can you turn the game to your advantage?

athletics

These sports are self-motivated and demand personal strength and power, and dreams about them can be representative of your drive and determination. Are you racing ahead and on a winning streak? Or is your dream suggesting that you slow down so that others can catch up with you? Are you lagging behind, with everyone else overtaking you? Ask yourself where in your waking life you feel the same.

travel

Travel and transport represent your journey through life. Travel can also represent the need to get away from it all and the desire to escape from your current situation. If you have a dream involving travel, consider what your journey is like. Is it a bumpy ride or plain sailing? What are the landscape and weather like? What is your means of transport? Are you walking barefoot to your destination on a bed of thorns, or are you being chauffeured there in a limo?

walking

A dream about walking suggests that in your waking life you take your time and go at your own pace. There's no need to be rushed or to be influenced by anyone else. The route you take within your dream and what happens on your journey will be relevant to your waking life in some way.

 **Terry's dream:** *I'm walking with my family in the country and it's a lovely, lazy day. The next thing I know, I'm alone and the path is getting rocky and I'm cold. I'm walking up a mountain and the top is covered in snow. I'm frightened and then I start to fall and fall. The shock wakes me up.*

Interpretation: Terry had applied for his dream job in America. In the meantime, he felt as if he was strolling though life. Then the letter arrived, offering him the post he'd been hoping for. Within an instant, his whole life changed – as reflected in his dream. In truth, he was terrified about leaving the life he knew and convinced that he would fail in the new job. Falling off the mountainside signified this fear.

Resolution: Terry's dream was mirroring his insecurities and fears, but thankfully, once they were out in the open, he was able to rationalise them. He realised that he was well qualified for the job and was likely to be able to do it well. He accepted the offer and left for America.

climbing

This dream suggests that something in your life may require an extra bit of effort. Does your life feel like an uphill struggle? Notice whether you succeed in your effort to climb the mountain in your dream. What does this say about the way you tackle the 'mountains' in your life?

skateboarding

Skateboarding requires great skill and determination to master. There are many bumps and falls along the way, and you constantly have to pick yourself up off the ground. Once you have mastered the skateboard, however, you can rise above any obstacle with style, flair, daring and enthusiasm. Consider where in your life you can do the same.

cycling

You can cover a considerable amount of distance on a bicycle. Again, this dream suggests that you are in control and can go at your own pace through life. Take note of the changing scenery in your dream. If your bike has a puncture, this could imply a short delay in a current project.

driving and cars

How do you see yourself in life? Are you a vintage car type of person, stylish and classy? Do you prefer to trundle along slowly in an old banger, or are you a boy racer with a flashy red sports car? If the latter, you probably like to be noticed and thought of as a sex symbol. Take note of any car in your dream and consider its qualities and how they relate to you. The colour of the car may also be important (see section on Colours, page 129).

To girls, cars are often a status symbol and an object of ambition, whereas to boys they may represent manliness, sexual prowess, and drive and determination.

trains

Train journeys represent your own unique passage through life. In your dream are you waiting at the station for a train that never arrives? Does this represent your frustration and eagerness to get on with life? What changes can you make to get things going again? Are you on a fast hi-tech train, racing through life and getting exactly where you want to be, or is the train speeding away out of control? If the latter, what aspect of your life feels as if it is rushing onwards and out of your hands? Does the train forget to stop at your station? If so, consider whether your life is on the right track. How can you make changes to get back on course?

aeroplanes

Planes are the fastest mode of transport and represent a quick route and direct access to what you want in life. If you dream about a plane and none of the above seems relevant, ask yourself whether you need a holiday.

bridges and walkways

Both bridges and walkways are links taking you from one place to another. They represent changes ahead and decisions to be made on the way to fresh horizons.

Is the bridge in your dream firm and solid, implying that no matter how difficult your journey, you will be supported along the way? If your bridge is a flimsy rope ladder – such as in the film *Indiana Jones and the Temple of Doom* – your journey may be fraught with danger and pitfalls and requires caution and extra care. On the other hand, the rope ladder may represent your fears and anxieties about something in your life. Changes in life can, indeed, be frightening, but the very nature of life is challenge and opportunity, and standing still is rarely the best option. Face the fear, trust in fate and do it anyway. Remember that Indiana Jones did get to the treasure in the end!

abstract themes

This grouping contains more general concepts. Nevertheless, these themes can have very great significance in a dream and can help to unlock its meaning for you.

colours

Why do some people dream in colour and others in black and white, and does it matter? This is a question that is often asked. The answer really depends on your personality and how you think in your waking life. If you are a creative character and have an artistic temperament, you are much more likely to dream in colour. If you are a logical thinker with an analytical type of brain, it's likely that you will dream in black and white. Most people are not aware of colours in their dream at all and dream in a murky twilight zone of misty grey.

The colour in your dream becomes important only if you feel it is significant yourself and if it stands out. Steven Spielberg, one of the world's most renowned film directors, used colour imagery very poignantly in his award-winning film *Schindler's List*. The whole film was shot in black and white with one exception. A little girl was seen running through the streets wearing a red coat. The four-year-old girl was a Jewish child, Roma Ligocka, who experienced the terrors of the Krakow ghetto during the Second World War. The red coat was a symbol of all the children who were murdered by the Nazis. Red symbolises blood – the blood of death and the blood of life; it also symbolises the will to survive. In real life, this little girl was one of a very few Jewish children to survive the holocaust. She escaped the ghetto only because she looked so pretty in her lovely red coat, which charmed a Polish girl, who offered her shelter from the Nazis.

If upon waking from your dream you can recall a specific colour, and you have a sense of it being important, then it surely is. Below is a list of colours and some of their universal meanings, although you will find that different colours are regarded differently in different cultures – for example, to the Irish, green is lucky, but to the Chinese, red is the lucky colour. Remember that your dream is unique to you, and a colour may trigger a thought in your mind that is more significant than the interpretations below.

- **Black:** Chic stylishness, depression, negativity
- **White:** Purity and innocence, coldness and iciness, cleanliness
- **Red:** Passion, lust and desire, sex and sexuality, the blood of life and of death, anger and rage, stop signs – as in traffic lights
- **Deep pink:** Love and femininity
- **Pale pink:** Female energy, intuition, care, earth-connected spirituality, baby girls
- **Yellow:** Inspiration, clarity of thought, education, the sun, optimism. (Try wearing something yellow if you are taking an exam or driving test.)
- **Orange:** Opulence and luxury, energy and fun, peace and harmony
- **Green:** Go signs, nature, money, envy, jealousy, good luck
- **Blue:** Masculine energy, thought and communication, ambition and drive
- **Indigo blue:** Tranquillity, higher thought
- **Purple:** Spirituality, the gods, royalty, ceremony
- **Silver:** The moon, feminine intuition
- **Gold:** The sun, wealth and riches, male energy, drive and ambition, physical activity

You need different energies for different situations; the use of colours can help you create the correct mood for the occasion. For example, if you are a woman and going for an interview in a bank, blue clothes would be more appropriate than pink.

cartoon imagery

I have never experienced this type of dream, but I know from the many dreams that are sent to me by teenagers that a lot of you do dream in animation and cartoon imagery; this must be an amazing experience. Sometimes the whole of the dream is animated, or sometimes one person or object in the dream turns into a cartoon character – as in the film *Roger Rabbit*. This type of dream is highlighting humour and the funny side of a given situation and may signify that you are prepared to take a light-hearted view of things. Who is the central cartoon character in your dream? Who does this character relate to in your waking life? Are they less frightening as a cartoon figure? Are they a caricature? Dreaming in this way is also a strong sign of artistic creativity.

Andrew's dream: *I'm walking down a street with a few of my mates. Coming towards us is a group of guys who we don't know. They look pretty mean. We walk up to each other slowly, but when they get close to us they turn into marshmallow men and start floating up in the air.*

Interpretation: Andrew had moved house and was starting a new school. He was finding this difficult as he missed his friends and thought he would never make new ones. He thought the lads in his class were tough and did not like him.

Resolution: Andrew's dream was telling him to chill out, see the funny side of his situation and give the new guys in his class a chance. It turned out that they weren't as intimidating as he thought; in fact they were just full of hot air!

numbers

Numerology is an ancient science concerned with the power of numbers. Pythagoras held the view that each digit resonates at a certain vibration and has an influence on the world around us.

If a number appears to you in a dream it certainly is worth paying attention to it. Try using it as your lucky number.

Although numbers have a universal symbolic meaning, it is important to remember that a number could have a significance to you alone, and you should always consider this personal meaning first. Is the number in your dream the same as the number of a house you used to live in? Why is that important? Does the number relate to something or someone in your life? Did your granddad once drive the number 17 bus for instance? Try to link the number or numbers to anything significant in your life before referring to the universal meanings below.

- **One:** The self, being the best or number one, indivisibility

- **Two:** Duality and balance, partnerships, male and female, being second best

- **Three:** The Trinity; mind, body and spirit; creativity

- **Four:** The four seasons, the square, stability and foundations

- **Five:** A mystical and psychic number, the pentacle (the five-pointed star of the occult), the five senses

- **Six:** The family unit, education, health

- **Seven:** Magic, supernatural powers, instinct and intuition, seventh heaven. There are seven colours in the spectrum and seven notes in the musical scale.

- **Eight:** Honesty, hard work and loyalty, wealth and success

- **Nine:** Art and creativity – a lucky number for actors and writers

- **Ten:** Inner wisdom, completion

- **Eleven:** Dynamism, spirituality. The number 11 has proved significant throughout history, for example, Remembrance Day (the 11th day of the 11th month) and September 11th.

𑅑 **Thirteen:** Bad luck for some, good luck for others. This number is indivisible.

𑅑 **Twenty-two:** This number has always been considered to have magical significance.

how to work out your lucky number

Say you were born on 23 October 1986 – that's 23.10.1986.
If the day has two digits, add them together:
23:    2 + 3 = 5
If the month has two digits, add them together:
10:    1 + 0 = 1
Add the year numbers together:
1986: 1 + 9 +8 + 6 = 24
If the total has two digits, add them together:
24:    2 + 4 = 6
Add the day, month and year numbers:
5 + 1 + 6 = 12
If the total has more than one digit, add them together:
12:    1 + 2 = 3
Your lucky number is 3.

horoscopes

I'm often asked if your zodiac sign can influence your style of dreaming. The 12 signs of the zodiac are divided into the four elements of fire, water, air and earth, and it is logical to presume that if you're a fire sign your subconscious will send you dream symbols relating to fire, for example dreams characterised by red, images of fires burning and so on. However, this is not always the case.

My own experience is in fact exactly the opposite. I am a fire sign, with the strong qualities of Leo the lion, and by nature have a fiery personality. You would imagine that my dreams would be filled with fire images, but this is not so; my dreams almost always speak to me in the language of water. I find that water calms me down and redresses the balance of my fiery temperament. When I started to think about the influence of star signs in dreaming, I began to notice some interesting facts about my life; you may be able to see similar patterns in yours.

I have chosen to live by the sea, and I also have a considerable amount of water around me, such as ponds and fountains. My partner in life was born under a water sign. I think if I lived with another fire sign we would be constantly at battle. In my working environment, which is artistic and creative, I love working with other fire signs; we spark off each other and fire each other's enthusiasm. Air signs also light my fire and I find them exciting to be around. On the other hand, people who are earth signs tend to bring me back down to earth with a bump, and water signs definitely put my fire out where work is concerned.

What is the element of your star sign and how does your dream language speak to you? Does your dream language communicate to you in the language of your element, or, like mine, does it tend to contradict your element? Consider your star sign and those of your family and close friends. Discover what type of people you work best with. Are they different from the people you choose to have fun and relax with? What type of person might you like to share your life with?

⟩⟩ **Fire language:** Fires and burning, standing around bonfires, torches, candles, the colour red, feelings of heat and warmth, forest fires, heated arguments, aggressive fighting, being trapped in burning buildings, explosions

⟩⟩ **Earth language:** Trees, mountains, woodland, plants and nature, digging in soil, gardening, earthbound animals, being trapped underground, being lost in a maze

⟩⟩ **Water language:** Bathing, swimming, the sea, the beach, paddling, drinking, waterfalls, rivers and streams, boating, rain, tidal waves, drowning

⟩⟩ **Air language:** Wind, breezes, kites, flying, storms, hurricanes and tornadoes, breath and breathing

If you dream of the signs of the zodiac, consider the qualities and characteristics below. How do they relate to your life?

Aries ♈

🜺 **Dates:** 21 March to 20 April

🜺 **Element:** Fire

🜺 **Symbol:** The ram

🜺 **Positive qualities:** Independent, courageous, natural leader, good in business and money matters

🜺 **Negative qualities:** Aggressive, egotistical, jealous, have to have their own way

Taurus ♉

🜺 **Dates:** 21 April to 21 May

🜺 **Element:** Earth

🜺 **Symbol:** The bull

🜺 **Positive qualities:** Down to earth, strong connection with nature, modest and understanding, kind, loyal

🜺 **Negative qualities:** Stubborn, slow to make decisions, creature of routine, lack of self-belief

Gemini ♊

🜺 **Dates:** 22 May to 21 June

🜺 **Element:** Air

🜺 **Symbol:** The twins

🜺 **Positive qualities:** Bubbly, charming, full of fun, generous, kind, enthusiastic

🜺 **Negative qualities:** Dual personality, changeable, moody, lack of concentration

Cancer ♋

 **Dates:** 22 June to 22 July

 **Element:** Water

 **Symbol:** The crab

 **Positive qualities:** Homely, constructive, good at business, kind, broad views, large interests, trustworthy

 **Negative qualities:** Worrisome, lonely, withdrawn

Leo ♌

 **Dates:** 23 July to 23 August

 **Element:** Fire

 **Symbol:** The lion

 **Positive qualities:** Magnetic personality, big thinker, full of fun and spirit, born leader, creative and flamboyant, nature lover, mischievous, courageous

 **Negative qualities:** Easily bored, over-protective, jealous

Virgo ♍

 **Dates:** 24 August to 23 September

 **Element:** Earth

 **Symbol:** The virgin

 **Positive qualities:** Home-lover, tidy, good communicator, good writer, logical

 **Negative qualities:** Fussy, lack of confidence, gossipy, untrusting

Libra ♎

 **Dates:** 24 September to 23 October

Element: Air

Symbol: The scales

Positive qualities: Love of beauty, strong intuition, sensitive, thoughtful, uncomplicated

Negative qualities: Timid, hide their feelings, obsessively tidy

Scorpio ♏

Dates: 24 October to 22 November

Element: Water

Symbol: The scorpion

Positive qualities: Courageous, confident, good judgement, keen to please, compassionate, hard-working

Negative qualities: Expect the worse, complicated emotions, vindictive and spiteful

Sagittarius ♐

Dates: 23 November to 21 December

Element: Fire

Symbol: The archer

Positive qualities: Good-hearted, good communicator, gets things done, natural wit, adventurous, good leader, good at selling and PR

Negative qualities: Superficial, flirtatious, bad-tempered

Capricorn ♑
- **Dates:** 22 December to 20 January

- **Element:** Earth

- **Symbol:** The goat

- **Positive qualities:** Hard-working, independent, good manager, ambitious and adaptable

- **Negative qualities:** Aloof, withdrawn, won't be hurried, sticklers for own routine

Aquarius ♒
- **Dates:** 21 January to 19 February

- **Element:** Air

- **Symbol:** The water carrier.

- **Positive qualities:** Natural leader, fascinating personality, full of original ideas, creative, open-minded, good communicator

- **Negative qualities:** Quirky personality, cranky and eccentric behaviour

Pisces ♓
- **Dates:** 20 February to 20 March

- **Element:** Water

- **Symbol:** The fish

- **Positive qualities:** Attractive, generous, sincere, magnetic, intuitive, charming

- **Negative qualities:** Rude, secretive, think too deeply, at odds with themselves, indecisive

Learning to Remember Your Dreams

Everybody dreams every night, but remembering your dreams is another matter. Memories of dreams are at their clearest just as you come out of sleep and before you fully wake up, a state that lasts only a few moments. Sometimes such a dream memory can be so vivid that it will stay with you for days, even years, but it's more likely that your dream will fade from your memory as soon as you're up and about.

However, in order to use your dreams to improve your life, you need to learn to remember them, and it's quite possible to do that. The most important thing that will help you is wanting to learn – it's as simple as that.

For most of us, as soon as we wake up, the mechanics of the day tend to take over. Click, the bedroom light is on and you're in action, getting dressed, snatching a bit of breakfast and out of the door. There are a million and one things to do, places to go, people to see – not enough time to fit everything into one day. The pace of life is fast and furious – you certainly don't have the time to ponder on what your dream was last night!

So what can you do if you want to remember your dreams? Simply get into the habit of writing them down. You just need to do a bit of preparation and make it a habit – habits are much harder to break than principles! Learning to remember your dreams takes a little practice and patience but is a highly rewarding experience.

getting ready

Of course, all you really need is a scrap of paper and a blunt pencil by the bed – but we can do better than that – and get better results!

First, set your alarm clock five or ten minutes earlier than you need. If someone else gives you a call in the morning, ask them to do so a few minutes earlier than usual to allow you enough time to make your dream notes. That way you will have a few minutes dedicated to jotting down the details of your dreams.

If you don't already have a bedside lamp, add it to your Christmas or birthday list just in case you wake up from a dream when it's still dark – as it will be on winter mornings in particular. Having to get out of bed to turn on the light could break your flow of concentration.

Before you go to bed, make sure you have a pencil and paper ready by your bed. Even better, you can create a dream diary – of which, more later – or you can make a few photocopies of the dream worksheet on pages 160–1 and keep these by your bed. They will also prompt you on things to try to remember about your dream, and you can jot words and images from your dream into the appropriate boxes.

If necessary, allocate another few minutes during or at the end of the day to filling in some more of the dream details so that you have a more complete record.

preparing for better dream recall

In ancient times, preparation for dreaming was taken very seriously indeed. Days were spent in fasting and meditation, and trance-like states were induced to encourage dreaming. I don't advise any of this, of course, but you can do some simple practical things that you may find helpful in making you relaxed and able to sleep well – and dream well, too!

You need to feel relaxed when you go to bed. Enjoy a warm, fragrant bath to help you wind down from the physical and mental stresses of the day – lavender and ylang ylang are great for relaxing, so put some bath oil or bubbles on that present list. Try reading for a short while before going to sleep. This often helps to put you in the right frame of mind for sleep and stops you churning over the day's events in your mind. Avoid eating too late, as this can overwork your body and disrupt your sleep. Also, make sure you're not too exhausted.

As you drop off to sleep, make sure you relax your mind as best you can. Close your eyes and say to yourself: 'I am going to remember my dream in the morning.' It's as simple as that.

There's a half-way stage that you may go through before falling properly asleep. I'm sure you will have experienced this many times. It's a dreamy, cosy feeling that is neither awake nor asleep, a state where images and ideas drift through your mind. This is in fact a state of hypnosis known as hypnogogic. When you enter this state, you can ask your subconscious mind to find solutions to any problems you might need help with. Ask it to send you a dream that will be helpful to you. If you are over-tired you will skip this stage and drop straight off to sleep.

waking up

In the morning, just before fully waking up, you enter the same hypnotic state. You are neither fully awake, nor are you asleep. Again, this is a cosy, dreamy stage where it feels as though your mind is floating. This is where you can recall your dreams most clearly. If you rush out of bed too quickly you will skip this stage and are likely to forget your dreams.

When you're aware that you're starting to wake up, keep your eyes closed and try not to move. Stay for as long as you can in this half-way stage and let thoughts and images come into your mind. Try to recall your dream. Go through as much of it as possible and then, when you feel ready, *slowly and calmly* reach for your pen and start to write down your dream and any other thoughts that come into your mind. Don't try too hard, because the harder you try to remember, the more elusive dreams can become.

making your dream notes

As soon as you wake up, when your dream images are clearest, jot down the gist of your dream – you may want to do this on rough paper in the first place. Write down immediately whatever words or images come into your mind and don't be concerned if they don't make any sense right away. You only need a few minutes but it should be quality time dedicated to going through your dream in your mind and writing down as much as possible of what you remember. Having to jump straight out of bed and start getting ready for the day will hinder the process. There's no need to write an epic storyline – just keep to the main points.

Make sure you include the date; remember your dreams relate directly to your waking life, so things that are happening to you every day will affect both what you dream and how you interpret it. You may want to fill in that information in advance.

Another alternative is to record your notes on a tape. Do whatever feels right for you.

Some of you may want to write everything down straightaway; others may prefer to find some time during the day to fill in the details. Do try to write down as much of your dream as you can as soon as possible afterwards, though. Dreams are very good at escaping! However, you don't always need to remember all of your dream to work out its message. You may need only a few images to make sense of the dream.

You can also make notes during the day on your day-dreams. These often define your innermost goals and so can be very enlightening when you look at the patterns that emerge from them.

interpreting your dreams

The perfect time to read through your dream and work out its meaning is when the bustle of the day is over and your mind is winding down, relaxing and preparing for sleep and another night's adventures. Record your interpretation in the same place as your dream notes so that you have a complete record. You may find that throughout the day your dream has kept coming back into your mind and by bedtime you have already worked out its meaning.

Once you start writing down your dreams on a regular basis, you will soon have a fascinating insight into your inner world. You will in time be able to look back at some of your more profound dreams and identify patterns emerging that show you how you think, how you feel, what you love, what you are afraid of, how you react and how you adjust to situations in your life. You will certainly get to know yourself better and learn more about what makes you tick.

You can refer to your dreams for guidance and inspiration with each new project. Your written dreams will be a vast treasure trove of your life – past, present and future.

your dream diary

Pencil and paper will do fine to keep your dream notes, as will a note book, but better still make your own private dream diary. You can write all your dreams in it or just the special and important ones. You can write straight into the book, or jot down notes on paper or in a note book, then write them up later. You can keep your dream diary for years and look back on it over time; a dream diary can be something you treasure and will be an inspiration for you when you are older.

Buy yourself a hard-backed exercise book, the thicker the better. Write on the front cover 'Night Dreams'. To make your book special and unique, decorate the front cover with images of how you imagine or would like your dream world to be. You can find cuttings of dragons, flying saucers, monsters, spells and magic – whatever feels good to you. Make your diary magical, mysterious, exciting and fun; this way you will want to use it.

When you have decorated the front cover to your liking, close the book and turn it upside down and back to front. This is going to be your day-dream book! Write on this (back) cover the title 'Day-dreams'. Once again, paste or draw pictures on the cover that inspire and motivate you. Make it as wild and exciting as you can. Remember that your day-dreams are preparing you for your life's path, so find or draw pictures of how you would like your future life to be. For example, you could have a drawing of you landing on the planet Mars, standing on the set of *EastEnders* or presenting your own television programme. Go on, let your imagination fly free.

Whichever way up you are using the book, use only the right-hand page to write down your dreams. That way, the book will be easier to write in, and you can read something interesting and inspiring whichever way you look at it! Mark the date, then describe your dream or day-dream. You could start with just an outline at the top to remind you of what the dream was about – jot that down when you wake up – and then fill the page with details you recall later on.

When, years later, you go back to your dream diary – as you sip your champagne in your Beverly Hills mansion – you can remind yourself of how you conquered those obstacles to arrive at a scenario you once only dreamed of. They can come true, you know!

your prompt list

The worksheet on pages 160–1 shows you the type of questions you should be asking about your dream in order to remember and interpret it. Some examples are:

- Who was in your dream?
- How were you feeling?
- Were there any objects or animals in your dream?
- What was happening?
- What was the setting/landscape like?
- What was the atmosphere like?
- Were there any significant colours in your dream?
- What was the event?

As long as you have answered as many of the questions on the prompt list as you can, you should have enough information to work out the meaning of your dream.

There is also space on the worksheet to add details about what's going on in your life at the time.

what if I can't remember my dreams?

As we have already noted, everyone dreams, but not everyone remembers their dreams. If you find that you cannot recall your dreams even after a time of trying, it doesn't mean you don't dream; it usually just means that you are waking up in a non-REM stage of sleep.

If this is the case, you can try an alternative approach. Set your alarm for a different time from usual – half an hour earlier or later. You could perhaps do this at weekends when you don't have to get up for school, college or work. If you still have no joy, try an hour earlier or later. If you're still not getting any results and you really need to prove to yourself that you do dream, then set your alarm for three hours after you go to bed. This will be about the time in your sleep pattern when you enter your second phase of REM sleep.

In the unlikely event that you still have no success, try an experiment with a friend. This, of course, will have to be a good friend as you will be asking them to stay awake while you are sleeping; you could offer to do the same for them. They need to watch your eyes and wake you up when you enter REM sleep – remember that in REM (rapid eye movement) sleep, your eyes will be closed and moving very quickly as if you are following something. If you are woken up while this is happening, you will most certainly be able to recall some of your dreams. At least this will prove to you that you do dream. It's not actually harmful to be woken up during REM sleep, but don't forget that having disturbed sleep of any kind can make you ratty and bad-tempered in the morning! It's certainly not something you should try on a regular basis.

Let's Interpret Your Dreams

The worksheet on pages 160–1 is designed for you to copy or photocopy to help you gather the most useful information about your dreams when you wake up. Fill in the boxes as quickly as you can, taking words, images and other notes directly from your dream. Fill in as many sections as you can before you sit back and try to interpret your dream.

When you are filling in the worksheet, let your mind roam freely. Try to do it quickly and without attaching too much thought to it. If you think too hard, your logical brain will kick into gear and this is what you want to avoid. You are dealing with your subconscious mind here, and logical thinking will more than likely take you down the wrong track. Keep your mind open and relaxed, and write down the first thing that comes into your head *regardless* of what it is. You may have been looking at a garden gate and yet write down 'prison', but there will be a reason for this. Perhaps a garden gate reminds you of being locked in, trapped or in prison. If you let your logical mind think about the garden gate, it will start to dismiss your first instinctive thoughts. Let your thoughts just pop up and, if you can, leave your rational thinking out of this exercise.

are you in the dream?

Make a note if you appear as yourself within your dream, but also be aware of any differences there might be. For example, you may be wearing clothes that you would not normally wear or doing something you would not normally do.

If you don't see yourself (as your waking self) in the dream, this may be because you're not appearing as yourself. If this is the case, don't be concerned – it's very normal. You are, however, likely to be represented somewhere. You may have a sense of yourself watching the scene, as if you were watching the TV. Even if the dream has no one in it at all, it may still contain objects that symbolise you. It may seem a bit tricky at first to work out the dream language, but once you have the knack of it, you can make lots of explorations into your own psyche.

\\\ **Me in a dream:** Let's say your dream is of a snow scene at night. It's very dark and you feel frightened. You're experiencing the sensation of being afraid even though you're not in the scene.

\\\ **Interpretation:** The main feeling you are experiencing in the dream is fear, but you don't know what's causing that fear. If you look up snow in a dream interpretation book, it may give the meaning 'innocence', but this is probably not relevant to the scene in this dream. Your snow scene is cold and dark, and you are afraid. So let's stick to these few clues. As there is no one in the scene and the landscape appears deserted, it would be safe to suggest that there could be a feeling of loneliness and isolation. I would ask whether there is any aspect of your life in which you are feeling cut off from people, isolated and out in the cold. Perhaps these feelings are so unpleasant that they frighten you. Can you see my train of thought here?

\\\ **Resolution:** You would need to think about how all of this applies to your life, and then take some action to change the situation, such as joining a club where you can make new friends, for example.

people you know

Make a list of the people in the dream who you know. Write down the first thoughts that come into your head about them. Let your mind roam freely and just jot down a few words – such as 'nasty', 'beautiful', 'arrogant', 'unkind', 'sympathetic' and so on.

people you don't know

Write down a brief description of any people you don't know. Again, without thinking too deeply about it, jot down any words that immediately come to mind – 'sexy', 'gorgeous', 'big-headed', 'piercing eyes'.

animals

If there are animals in your dream, make a note of them. Your subconscious mind may be sending you a message by using the characteristics of an animal.

objects

Any significant object in your dream will have a meaning or message. The object could represent you, or it could represent your feelings or your attitude. Let's look at a simple object such as a table, for example. A table is used to support other objects. It could be a dining table with food on it; it could be a work table that has DIY tools on it; it could be a desk. Any of these different kinds of table could be representing a part of your life.

A desk in a dream: Let's say that a prominent feature in your dream is a desk and it's laden down with 'stuff'. There are heaps of books on it, stacks of discarded toffee papers, three computers, CDs and all kinds of other things. The overall look of the desk is a shambles; it's overloaded and it would be impossible to sit and do any work at it.

\\\ **Interpretation:** Perhaps you are the desk and you are overloading yourself with too much work. The dream could be suggesting that you clear the clutter out of your life and reorganise yourself before you collapse under the weight of all this 'stuff'.

\\\ **Resolution:** Well, it's pretty obvious, isn't it? Take a broom to the clutter in your work life – and perhaps also your emotional life if clutter is an issue there too.

situation and environment

Where are you in your dream? Are you inside a building, or are you outside, perhaps walking by a deserted beach? Are you flying through the air or just about to land on the moon? Take a look at what is immediately around you and then consider your wider environment. What era is it? Are you in the present? Have you gone back to a time when dinosaurs rule the planet? Or are you sitting your driving test, which is next week? Is it somewhere you know, such as your parents' house, or are you in a strange landscape? Is the place bright and warm? Do you feel comfortable there? Is it dark and dirty? Jot down a few words that sum up where you are in your dream.

\\\ *Let's Interpret Your Dreams*

event

What is happening or about to happen in your dream? Write a little about what's going on.

what is the action?

Are you swimming, driving, being driven, standing and watching? Write down what actually happens in the sequence in which it happens, if you can.

what is the atmosphere like?

Is the atmosphere in your dream tense or relaxed? Do you have a sense that something is about to happen? This is all-important to the final interpretation of your dream.

how do you feel?

You may feel in harmony with the dream, or you may feel strange. For example, the setting of the dream might be a very tense one – such as the scene of a car accident – but you may feel cool, calm and collected, and be dealing competently with the situation while everyone and everything around you is in chaos. Alternatively, you could be walking on a beautiful beach surrounded by happy people but feeling anxious and on nervous alert. Make a note of how you are feeling; this is always relevant in your dreams.

colours

Are you dreaming in black and white or do any of the colours seem significant? If you can't remember, that's fine; only make a note of it if you feel it's important. For example, you may be driving along a country road and you know for certain you are in a bright red sports car – no other colour stands out at all. In this situation the colour is likely to have some significance.

what's happening in your life?

Let's now come out of the dream and take a look at your waking life. Your dream world is sending you a message for a reason: there's an issue that your subconscious mind would like you to look at and possibly do something about, so your current situation will certainly be relevant in some way. Is there an event coming up in the near future that you are thinking, worrying or hoping about? Your dream could be bringing up an old issue that happened some time in the past but that may be affecting your present situation.

Look at what's going on currently in your life. What's happening in your love life, your working life, your family life? What plans are you making for the immediate future? How have you been feeling lately? Are you happy, excited or depressed and what is making you feel this way? What are you doing today and in the next few days? Again, without thinking too deeply, just jot down whatever comes into your head. You just may dismiss something important if you think too much about what you are writing.

Let's say, for example, you're going to college, you're seeing your friends at the weekend, you're going to the dentist on Thursday, you're waiting for a letter from a friend, you have to clean your bedroom and you want to buy a new jacket. Going to the dentist ... Oh dear, going to the dentist ... Alarm bells! You might dismiss something as trivial as going to the dentist because on the surface it doesn't appear to be anything exciting or important, but it may be that in your subconscious you are very anxious about it.

interpreting from your worksheet

The chances are that the very process of writing down all those thoughts and feelings has already helped you to work out what your dream is about. If not, then slowly read through your worksheet and at the same time look at what's happening in your current life. Does anything obviously link up? First, look at the feelings you experienced in your dream and consider how they relate to any situation in your waking life. If you get the 'aha!' feeling, then ... Eureka! You've got it!

worksheet examples

Now let's look at worksheets filled in by Holly (age 14) and Liam (age 15) to see how the process works with real dreams.

In practice, Holly and Liam would have jotted down their notes at the top of the worksheet and then extracted the information to put in the relevant boxes in the second column of the worksheet. They would then start to interpret the individual elements by filling in the last column before moving on to a conclusion. For the sake of clarity, however, in these examples I have gone through the dreams one stage at a time.

Holly's dream interpretation worksheet

Date: 23 February 2003

Dream notes: *I'm riding my bike down a cobbled country lane. It's a bit bumpy so I have to go pretty slowly. I pass my old school and I notice there's a lot of excitement going on. There's a group of boys and girls dressed in bright football kits. They're shouting and having a lot of fun. It feels as though they're getting ready to play football – a match I think, as they're so excited. I notice that the large metal school gates are locked, which makes me feel sad. I start to wobble on my bike and have to concentrate to get going again. I have to pedal hard and fast to stay on. When I look up again, the school is gone and I'm back on the road. It's a hot summer day and I pedal into the sunshine. I feel OK, quite happy in fact.*

Topic	Dream details	Notes and comments
Me	*Holly.*	*This dream is about me.*
People I know	*Not really.*	
People I don't know	*Did not recognise any of them in particular, but they were sort of familiar.*	*The actual people in the dream represent the past rather than being individually important.*
Animals	*None.*	*Pupils from my old school.*
Objects	*Bicycle, school gates, football kit.*	*The school gates are locked and I'm on the outside. I can't go back to the old days. The bicycle represents my journey in life; I'm riding it and I'm in control.*

Let's Interpret Your Dreams

Topic	Dream details	Notes and comments
Situation and environment	Old cobbled country lane, old school.	The old cobbled lane suggests this is in the past.
Event	Waiting to play a match	
Atmosphere	I'm calm; the school kids are excited.	The kids in the playground are excited. At first I'm calm, and then I feel sad because I'm not with them.
Feelings	I felt a bit sad at seeing my old school and everyone having a great time. Then I felt happy on my bike, riding into the sunshine and countryside.	I'm sad at leaving my old school and all my friends.
Colours	Nothing stood out other than the bright sunshine	This dream feels thoughtful but very positive.
Action	Cycling, watching	I'm cycling and looking at my old school.
Events and relationships	I've been in my new house and new school about a year or so. I've settled in better than I thought. I've just got my first part-time job working in a café. I've just been picked for a part in the school play.	My past year has been busy and full of change. I've moved a long way from my old home to a new house and new school, and this has been a major life change for me. At times, it's been very difficult to deal with. This dream seems to have come at a major turning point. My life is looking up and I've got over the trauma of moving. I'm ready to move on and let go of the past, and I'm looking forward to whatever life has to offer.
Other notes		

\\\ **Interpretation:** *When we first moved house I really missed my old school and all my friends. We'd moved a long way away and I knew I would never be able to keep in touch with my friends. I've got used to my new school now and things are beginning to feel good. I've just started a new part-time weekend job so I can earn some money, which feels great, and I've made some new friends too. I've also been chosen to be in the school play, which is really cool.*

\\\ **Resolution:** *My new life is going well. It's time to let go of my old school and my old friends and get on with the exciting things that are happening around me now.*

the message of this dream

This dream suggests that Holly is ready to let go of the past and reassures her that it's just fine for her to do so. She is no longer distressed by her move, even though it still makes her sad when she thinks of the past. The future is bright and positive and she has a lot to look forward to. She is now in the driving seat and in control of her life. This is a very positive dream about her future and her attitude towards it. She is ready to move forward in her life.

how to make use of this dream

Holly now knows that it's time to look ahead and not backwards. She can start to make plans in a positive way. One part of her life is over and she now feels OK about that. She has experienced a major life lesson and one that will repeat itself at certain times throughout her life. When another change in life happens, as it no doubt will, she will be able to deal with it with greater confidence.

Liam's dream interpretation worksheet

Date: 29 March 2003

Dream notes: *I'm trying to do something and when I look down at my hands I notice that my fingers are really fat and swollen. I begin walking but find that I'm in this dark underground bunker and I can hear people playing golf above me. It all feels a bit spooky.*

Topic	Dream details	Notes and comments
Me	Liam.	This dream is about me.
People I know	None.	
People I don't know	Men above me playing golf.	
Animals	None.	
Objects	Underground bunker, swollen fingers.	Underground bunker and swollen fingers.
Situation and environment	Dark bunker, golf course.	I'm stranded in a dark underground bunker.
Event	None	
Atmosphere	Dark and spooky.	Dark and spooky.
Feelings	A bit alarmed at my swollen fingers. Spooky in the dark and a bit frightening.	I'm alarmed about my fingers and spooked in the dark.
Colours	None, just dark.	
Action	Trying to do something with my hands, me walking, men golfing.	I'm trying to do something but my fingers are swollen. There are people above me playing golf.

Topic	Dream details	Notes and comments
Events and relationships	*I'm in my final year at school and am a prefect. I've just started a new subject, woodwork. I've got a girlfriend.*	*I'm a prefect at school and I work hard. I nearly always get A grades. I've just moved up into the final year and have taken on a couple of extra subjects. One of them is woodwork and I'm finding it very difficult. This is what my dream is really about – I can't deal with not being good at it. It's making me feel uncomfortable about everything else in my life.*
Other notes		

\\\ **Interpretation:** *I realise from writing down my dream that I really can't bear having to do something I'm not good at, and the woodwork is driving me mad. It's making me feel stupid and hopeless. It's starting to get me down. I feel as though everyone's laughing at me.*

\\\ **Resolution:** *I want to try to drop woodwork. I'm no good at it and I'm never going to be really good.*

the message of this dream

In his dream, Liam's fingers are swollen. This is what it feels like when he's doing woodwork. It's as though he can't hold anything or make his fingers do what he wants. The underground bunker represents his feelings of being 'in the dark' about his new subject. Above him are people playing golf; golf is a game of great skill, which it requires patience to develop. In this sense it is similar to woodwork. Liam will need to be patient if he is to acquire the skill to be a good woodworker.

how to make use of this dream

Liam was feeling hopeless at woodwork and was getting distressed about it. He felt that he was not good enough and that he would make a bad impression on everyone around him. His dream was trying to tell him that some things in life, such as golf and woodwork, take time and patience to perfect. After analysing his dream Liam wanted to drop woodwork, but after much torment he decided instead to change his attitude to it. He would make it a long-term project rather than a test he had to pass immediately. It's still hard for him to recognise that he doesn't need to be brilliant at everything, but he's now trying to do woodwork simply for fun and pleasure.

Your Dream Interpretation Workbook

You can copy these pages and use them to make notes on your dreams in the relevant spaces, then take a little time to note how they relate to your waking life – and what you are going to do to put the messages into action.

Date:

Dream notes:

≈ **Interpretation**

≈ **Resolution**

Topic	Dream details	Notes and comments
Me		
People I know		
People I don't know		
Animals		
Objects		
Situation and environment		
Event		
Actions		
Atmosphere		
Feelings		
Colours		
Events and relationships		
Other notes		

Dream Images

You know by now that dream images have to be related to your own experiences in order for you to make sense of them. However, some things have a general symbolic value which you can use to help you interpret your dreams. Remember also that images can have different meanings depending on their context, both in the dream itself and in your waking life.

a

abandoned: neglected, left behind

abortion: sad ending, unwanted, rejection

abroad: journey to new land, escape, travel away, strange situation, the unknown

abscess: situation about to burst, situation festering away

abuse: hostile, drugs, self-harm

accident: danger, warning

ace: the best, aim high, ambition, gamble

ache: hurt, pain, health, emotions

acrobat: juggling, flexibility

actor: limelight, skilled profession, pretence

adolescence: youth, awkwardness

adventure: need to escape, exciting times ahead

advert: announcement, making something known

aeroplane: need to escape, get away, quick advancement in life or work

affair: deceit, guilt

aggression: need to express anger, quarrel

agony: painful situation

alarm: warning bells, danger

alchemy: change, deception

alcohol: escapism, self-harm, abuse. *See* Alcohol (page 119)

alien: the unknown, hope

allergy: irritation, someone getting under your skin, worries

alone: isolation, need

altar: ritual, sacrifice, giving up of something

ambush: threat, under attack

angel: protection, guardian, support

angling: fishing for something, expectation

anorexia: denial, self-loathing, emotional starvation

ant: busy, hard work

antique: old-fashioned ideas, fragile, handle with care

appetite: hunger, need for nourishment

applause: reward, acknowledgement

apple: luscious, sexual, temptation

arch: doorway to change, support

archer: watch your back, precision, attention to detail

arm: support, grip

army: establishment, organised anger

arrow: clear thinking, the way ahead, target

art: freedom of expression

artist: expression, attention to detail

ashes: shattered hopes, disappointments, ending

asleep: escapism, lack of energy, ignorant, left in the dark

astrologer: guidance, advice

astrology: calculated planning

astronaut: escapism, adventure into the unknown, bravery

athletics: drive, competitiveness

atlas: travel plans, escape

attack: determination, desire, release of anger

attic: the future, wishes, desires

auction: competition, desire to succeed

audience: appreciation, acknowledgement, support

axe: split up, sever relationships with

b

baby: self nurturing, birth of new ideas and projects, new life, innocence

back: support, strength, someone out to get you

badge: reward, achievement

bag: hidden treasures, secrets

baldness: worries, concerns, fretting, virility
balloon: lighten up, celebration
balls: games, skill, masculinity
banana: nourishment, virility, phallic symbol
band: teamwork,
bandage: cover up, protect
bank: money concerns, protect your interests
baptism: ritual, membership, fresh beginning
bar: fun, social relaxation, celebration
barbecue: informal get together, relaxation
barking: need to express yourself, make yourself heard, alarm
barmaid: need to please others, need for attention,
    sexual subservience
basket: holding on, protecting, fear of loss, gathering
bat: inner fears, the occult
battle: prepare to fight, take action, self-beliefs
beach: recuperation, desire to get away, holiday
beans: new ideas, full of energy
beard: hiding behind something, disguise
beautician: self-image, need for improvement, attention
    to detail
beauty: image, ego, positive thinking
bed: need to rest, sexual desires
bees: busy time ahead, social habits
beggar: poverty, lack, in need of help
beheading: dramatic ending, new life, helplessness
bell: alarm, pay attention, take heed, announcement
belt: holding on, gather together, get a grip on
bet: risk, gamble, trust
bicycle: skill, control, journey through life
bill: pay-back time, asking for what is due
bin: rubbish, clutter-clearing, failed plans
bird: freedom, take flight
birth: new life being formed, new plans and projects
bite: get your teeth into something, bitten off more than you
    can chew
black: chic, sombre, in the dark. *See* Black (page 129)
blackboard: pay attention, notice

blackmail: guilt, shame, something to hide

blind: in the dark, what can't you see?

blonde: lighten up, change of attitude, act dumb

blood: the life force, death, fear, energy

blue: expect something out of the blue, depression. *See* Blue (page 129)

blushing: embarrassment, caught out

boat: support, travel. *See* Travel (page 125)

body: health, image

bomb: situation about to blow

bonfire: gathering, warning message, destruction

book: need to learn (consider the type of book)

boots: prepare for major changes, advancement

boss: person in authority, charge, control, own aspirations

bottle: party, escapism, addiction, what are you bottling up?

bouquet: acknowledgement, celebration, commiseration, reward

box: surprise, secrets

bracelet: commitment, partnership, shackles

bread: nourishment, sustenance, money

breast: mothering, need for tenderness, pregnancy, sexual desire

bribe: cheating, deception, getting what you want

bride: wedding, commitment, loss of virginity, new life

brothel: shame, sexual pleasures

bruise: hurt, sorrow, tenderness

bubble: protection

bud: tender new life, fresh ideas yet to unfold, gestation

bull: determination, stubbornness, strong, thick-skinned

burn: let go, trust, change, warning to keep away from a situation. *See* Fire themes (page 80)

bury: secret, need to hide

bus: waiting to move on, social journey close to home

butcher: take something apart, destroy in anger

butler: servitude, let someone else do the work for you

butterfly: change for the better, beauty, short-lived

buy: need, desire

C

cab: support, guidance, needing a lift in life

café: relax, chill out, social meeting place

cake: celebration, success

calculator: careful planning, what does not add up?

calendar: time issues, appointments, memories

camouflage: secrecy, disguise, under cover

camping: freedom, holidays

can: secrets locked away, discover the unknown, keeping safe

cancer: what is eating away at you?

candle: shed a light on, ritual, birthday celebrations, sexuality

canoe: navigate skilfully

cards: game of deception, trickery

castration: helplessness, hopelessness

cat: magic omen, stealth, secrecy, protection

catalogue: choices

caterpillar: temporary situation, ending, omen of new beginning, change. *See* Insects and creepy-crawlies (page 103)

cave: deep hidden feelings, solitude, feminine sexuality

cell: confined space, locked away

cellar: childhood memories good and bad, nostalgia, past secrets

cement: fixed in stone, contracts, solid agreements

certificate: reward, acknowledgement, sign of success

chain: bound, restrained, links

chair: support, comfort, position

champagne: celebration, success

chauffeur: being driven, being cared for, out of your control, trust in others

chef: preparation, gathering together, forward planning

cheque: financial improvement, luck, commitment

chess: care and thought in actions, game of skill and mental alertness

chewing: think something over, careful consideration, take your time

chicken: nerves, fear, cowardice, innocence

child: self-nurturing, protection, bringing out the child in yourself

chin: courage, taking a risk, bravery

chocolate: sensual pleasure, temptation, comfort

choir: part of a team, support, solidarity

cigar: pleasure, phallic symbol

cigarette: satisfaction, escapism

cinema: escape from routine, need to get away

circle: commitment, ongoing harmony, completion, trapped

circus: fiasco, unpredictability, fun

city: complexity, confusion

classroom: learning, knowledge

cleaning: desire to see, letting go of the old, making way for the new

cliff: difficult project

climbing: progress, determination, will to succeed

clock: time issues

clothing: ego, image. *See* Clothes (page 114)

cloud: obstruction, depression

clown: fun, relaxation, entertainment, sadness

clubbing: social escapism

coal: old knowledge, fuel needed for new project, good omen

cocaine: drugs, escapism, fear of facing reality

cockerel: boasting, big-headedness, pride

cocktail: fun, celebration, mixed feelings

coffee: energy booster, time to gather thoughts. *See* Tea and coffee (page 119)

coffin: passing of old ideas and situations, letting go, preparation for new life

coin: success, money issues

college: furthering knowledge, maturing

comedian: making fun of, lighten up

compass: need for direction, opportunities ahead

competition: desire to succeed

computer: skill, unlimited accessible information

condom: need for precaution, cover up

conductor: taking control, leadership

cooking: preparation of new plans

corkscrew: drive, determination, need for further information

corpse: the past, saying goodbye to outdated situations

costumes: pretending, covering up, falsehood

cot: place of safety, childhood protection

court: accountability, judgement, fairness

cow: mothering, nurturing

crab: devious, hiding, protection

cream: sensual pleasures, the best of, reward

crime: desire, the need to have

cripple: frustration, handicapped

crisps: treats

crossroads: choices, decisions, various options

crossword: need to work out problems, concentration

crow: omen, alarm, messenger of bad news

crowd: gathering, threatening

crown: reward, success, recognition

crucifix: sacrifice, helplessness

crying: releasing of emotions, sadness, joy, therapeutic

cup: if full denotes riches and rewards, if empty denotes lack

curry: combination, open-minded, exotic

curtain: obstruction, shield, unwilling to see, desire for solitude

cushion: soften the blow, protection, comfort

cut: open up secrets, reveal new information

d

dagger: threat, fear, revenge

dart: precision

death: ending of any situation, new start

defence: protection

degree: reward, acknowledgement, success

demolish: need to destroy, anger, resentment, ending

dentist: getting to the root of, image concerns

desert: reward, need for nourishment, comfort

desk: learning, knowledge, study

destruction: new beginnings

detective: secrets, discovery

devil: shame, disgust, guilt, sexual disgust

diamond: treasure, reward, celebration

dice: risk, gamble

diet: need for caution, restraint, starvation

digging: need for further knowledge, get to the bottom of

dinner: romantic meeting, family gathering, nourishment

diploma: success

dirt: guilt, shame

disaster: trauma, loss, letting go, fear of the future

disease: fear, concern, what is eating away at you?

divorce: separation, going it alone

doctor: need for attention, comfort, support

doll: childhood memories, plaything

dolphin: good luck, friendship, clear sailing ahead

donkey: stubbornness, plodding away, working hard

door: mouth, speech, gateway to new life, changes; closed door indicates secrets

dragon: protection, obstacles

drink: nourishment, celebration, quenching a thirst. *See* Drinks (page 119)

drive: in control, journey. *See* Driving and cars (page 127)

drowning: overburdened, under pressure

drum: alarm, warning, pay attention, announcement

dying: leaving behind the old, preparing for the new, letting go

e

eagle: power, freedom, high ideals, watchful

ear: listening, keep alert

earth: solid, dependable. *See* Earth themes (page 86)

earthquake: falling apart, unstable

eating: being fed, nourishment, need, hunger

echo: pay special attention to feedback from others

eczema: getting under your skin, irritation

electricity: unseen power

elevator: if ascending, success, elevation; if descending, a step backwards

engagement: commitment to new project

engine: drive, power, needs fuelling

envelope: secret, communication

erection: sexual power, manhood

eroticism: desire, pleasures of the flesh

evil: fear, the unknown, shame, guilt

exams: being held to account, testing

excrement: dumping your feelings

exercise: need for physical activity

exhibition: on show, exposed

expedition: new journey, plans, preparation needed

exploration: desire for further information

eye: be watchful, observe

eyebrows: protected, on guard, defence. *See* Eyebrows, (page 113)

f

face: image, mask

factory: hard work needed to succeed, busyness

fairy: deep wishes, protection, guardian, positive omen

falling: letting go, need to trust. *See* Falling (page 48)

fame: desire for, recognition, success

fancy dress: party, fun, deception

farmer: back to nature, growth, planning

fashion: image, acceptability

fat: self-revulsion, greed, comfort, abundance, protection

fate: trust

father: male figure of authority

fax: urgent message

feast: time of plenty, festivity, celebration

feathers: soft padding, protection, positive omen

fence: guarding, personal boundaries

ferry: leaving the old behind, journey into new phase of life

festival: celebration, success

fever: anger, need to let off steam

field: relaxation, back to nature, growth

fig: sexual image of fertility and male sperm

fight: confrontation

film: capture the moment, important memories

finger: who or what is it pointing at?

fitness: importance of exercise

flea: irritation, symbol of mighty power. *See* Biting and stinging insects (page 103)

flesh: protection, cover up, sexual desire

football: competition, team player

footballer: responsibility, in the public eye

fortune: success, greed

fountain: wealth, abundance, knowledge

fracture: split, rift in relationships, what is broken that needs mending?

freeze: frozen emotions, time to wait, on hold

frog: sexuality. *See* Frogs and toads (page 101)

frost: emotions turning cold, lean period ahead

fuel: energy

funeral: passing of a stage in life, new life about to begin, letting go

fur: protection, warmth

g

gale: storm brewing, disruption. *See* Air and weather (page 88)

gallows: fear, guilt, punishment, unwanted ending

gambling: risk, trust

games: competition, team spirit, desire to win, trickery

gang: fear of violence, threat

garage: repairs, fuel, what are you keeping under cover?

garden: growth, plans, projects

garlic: wards off evil spirits, cleansing, purifying, aphrodisiac

gate: opening, transition, change, opportunity

genie: positive omen, wishes coming true, help, support

genius: in control, all-knowing, confidence

ghost: doubts, the past, under pressure

giant: overpowering people, superiors, pride

gift: acceptance, receiving

gin: escapism, depression

glasses: look closer, scrutinise

gloves: sexual protection, untouchable, handle with care, discretion

glue: sticking together, repair, mend

goal: achievement, focus

god: authority, person in power, control, hope

gold: precious, reward, valuable. *See* Gold (page 129)

golf: game of skill, social status

graduate: achievement, recognition

grandparent: protector, wise person, family

grass: health, freedom, nature

grave: ending, the past, silence

guitar: creativity, sexual image

gun: aggression, protection, fear of attack, direction

gym: workout, physical exercise

gypsy: uncertainty, fear of the unknown, restlessness

h

hair: strength, image, ego

halo: wise, saintly

hammer: message, work to do

hand: support, ability

handbag: possessions, female privacy

handle: get a grip on things, support, entering the unknown

handshake: contract, agreement, new meeting

hanging: public humiliation, punishment

hangover: overindulgence, regrets

harbour: safety, refuge

harness: restriction, being held back

hat: image, making an impression; note the type of hat

headmaster: authority, paternal figure

headmistress: authority, maternal figure

health: health concerns, mirror of physical well-being

heart: powerhouse, driving force, love, desire

heat: need for warmth, too hot to handle

hedge: boundaries, privacy, boxed in

helicopter: quick get-away, adventure, skill, control

hell: fear, guilt, punishment

herbs: power of, medicinal

hero or heroine: cult figures, idol worship; note special qualities

hide: shame, deception, need for solitude

hill: climbing, progress, striving

holiday: need for holiday, desire to get away

home or house: security, foundations, family

honey: reward for hard work, sweet sensual pleasures

hood: disguise, deception, intimidation, under pressure

horoscope: hope, uncertainty about the future, trust, need for reassurance

horse racing: gambling, power, speed, excitement. See Games and sport (page 124)

horse: power, sexual prowess. *See* horses (page 98)

hosepipe: phallic symbol, wavering

hospital: need for care, attention, fixing, healing, recuperation

hotel: rest, escape from responsibility, travel

hunger: need for nourishment, attention

hunting: ruthless pursuit, greed, violence

hurdle: obstacles to get over, hindrances

hut: privacy, solitude, poverty

i

ice cream: treat, cool down, sexual connotations

icing: absolute pleasure, reward, dream come true

icon: admiration, worship; note the qualities

incense: ritual, setting a scene, sensual, pay homage to

indigestion: niggling concerns, irritation, what/who can't you stomach?

industry: hard work, getting stuck in, intensity

infant: childhood, memories from the past, nurturing yourself as you would a child

infection: feeling dirty, contaminated

infidelity: disappointment, shattered trust, suspicion

injection: care, sexual precaution

ink: formal agreement, communication

insects: fears, phobias. *See* Insects and creepie-crawlies (page 103)

intercourse: intimacy, close sharing, commitment, sexual desire, lust

interview: judgement, opportunity, being put on the spot

invasion: intrusion on privacy, abuse

invention: new ideas, plans, projects

invisible: need for attention, depression, feeling ignored, lonely

island: isolation, need for solitude, unapproachable

itch: irritation, getting under your skin, who/what is irritating you?

ivy: poison, choking, suffocating

J

jacket: protection, warmth, covering up

jail: trapped, confined, restricted

jam: treat, need for comfort, sticky, setting trap

jelly: shaky, afraid, feeling weak, fun

jester: ridicule, feeling foolish, take things less seriously

jigsaw: confusion, out of order, putting things in correct order

job: status, desire, work hard at

jockey: skilled control, power, excitement, sexual desire

jogging: driven, determined, keeping fit

joint: flexibility, drugs, escapism

journalist: flattery, attention, invasion of privacy

judge: fairness, just rewards, honesty, impartial figure, accountability

judo: personal strength, protection, controlled skill

juggling: too much to do, not enough time

juice: purity, concentration, essence of

jukebox: past memories, nostalgia

jumping: making major headway in life, quick advancement

jungle: wildness, raw energy, confusion, entangled web

jury: other people's opinions, being judged

k

karaoke: centre of attention, on show, enjoyment

karate: personal strength, protection

keep fit: personal health, exercise

kennel: in the dog house, being put in your place

key: solving a mystery, new projects

keyhole: opportunity, looking at your future

killing: ending, need to let go, fresh opportunity

king: authority figure, male, overpowering

kiss: sharing, sensuality, sex

kitchen: cooking up something, preparation, expectation. *See* Kitchens (page 122)

kite: freedom, as light as

kitten: protection, vulnerability

knee: flexibility, aggression

knitting: scheming, complications

knot: holding on too tightly, inseparable, something to remember

knuckle: aggression, force

l

label, designer: status, ego, need to impress, judging others

ladder: progress, going up in the world, escape

lady: gentle, softness, class, style

lame: obstacles, need for support, assistance

lake: still waters run deep, refreshment. *See* Water themes (page 74)

lamb: innocence, helpless

landlord: authority figure, intimidation

landscape: overall view, the bigger picture

language: skill, communication

laughing: make light of, see the funny side of

law: restrictions, conformity

leaflet: information, promotion

leaking: escaping energy, sapping your strength, need to cry

leather: tough skin, protection

leaves: health, vitality, new projects
lecture: domination, restriction
leg: support, prop, progress
lemon: tart, bitter, sharp, zest
letter: news
library: knowledge, study, seek information
licking: sensuality, wounded
lie: cover up, deceit, protection
lifeboat: coming to the rescue, safety after the storm
light: understanding, solve mystery, shedding light on
lighthouse: refuge, safety, guiding light
lily: honesty, respect
limousine: going up in the world, success, ego
lion: bravery, pride, honour, protection. *See* Lions (page 99)
lips: sensuality, sexuality
litter: clutter-clearing, get rid of
loneliness: need for friendship, isolation
lotto: luck, desperation, gamble
love: desire, partnerships
lovemaking: lust, sexuality, sexual frustration
lover: new relationship, sexual frustration, unfulfilled desire
luck: change of fortune
luggage: travel, moving on, holding on to personal
　　baggage, burdens

M

machinery: trapped in routine, precision
madness: confusion, overworked, need for rest
magazine: image, status, ego, profile
magic: you can make anything happen, expect the unexpected
make-up: deception, covering up, disguise, unexpected event
manicure: attention to detail, preparation
mansion: hope, aspiration, greed, lust for life
manure: back to basics, nourishment, growth
map: see a way forward, escape, make plans
market: be available, market yourself, investment
marriage: commitment, partnership, new deals

massage: pampering, deep thinking, getting to the bottom of

match: confrontation, arguments, battle

maths: work out, make plans, thoughtful consideration

maze: confusion, lost, anxiety

measure: careful planning, calculating, new plans afoot

medal: reward, recognition, personal achievement

medicine: tonic, come-uppance

meeting: joining of ideas, partnerships

melon: sensuality, sexual implications, ripe

mermaid: mythical creature, magic, good luck, sexual frustration, escapism

message: news, discussion

microphone: need to be heard

milk: nurturing, mothering

mine: dig deeper, hidden knowledge, treasure, exploring

minefield: danger, tread carefully

miracle: rescue, trust, acceptance, reward

mirror: honesty, truth, reality, vanity

mist: confusion, unclear, hidden from view

mobile phone: communication, urgent message

model: aspirations, perfection, image

mole: in the dark, not knowing

money: fortune, reward, unexpected gift

monkey: trickery, mischief

monster: inner fear, being overpowered, dominated, attacked. *See* Monsters (page 45)

moon: spiritual knowledge, intuition, guidance, menstruation

mortuary: letting go of the past, outworn ideas, new life

mosquito: little irritations, sucking the blood out of you, sapping your energy. *See* Biting and stinging insects (page 103)

moth: eating away at you, unseen damage

mother: maternal figure, need for nurturing, pregnancy

moustache: cover up, disguise, suspicion

mouth: need to speak, sensuality, new opening

mud: confusion, feeling stuck, unclear

mushroom: festering, being kept in the dark

music: relaxation, enjoyment, escapism

n

nails: fix, repair, being held together

naked: exposed, vulnerable, feeling confident

neck: risk, vulnerability

needle: question, delve into, repair, fix

nest: making home, comfort

net: hold on to, capture,

news: communication, expectancy

newspaper: take notice, announcement

nickname: take less seriously, endearment, tender, making fun of

night: in the dark, thoughtful, period of waiting

nightclub: fun, relaxation, escapism, sex

nose: sniff out, astute sense, inquisitive

notice: announcement, pay attention to

nun: sinister, demonic, saintly

nurse: need for attention, care, needy, sexual image

nursery: innocent play, security

nuts: saving, hoarding, nourishment, male genitals

O

oak: solid, strong, support, reliable, trustworthy. *See* Oak (page 93)

oath: promise, vow, commitment

office: organisation, routine, work

oil: wealth, lubricate, smooth running of

ointment: heal wounds, care, rub in

old: wisdom, quality, outdated, time to replace

olive: exotic, pleasure, peace, make amends

omelette: mixed up, confusion

onions: antiseptic, tears

opera: grand gestures, overstated, grand, elaborate, drama

opium: escapism, release, addiction, out of it

orchestra: fine tuning, team players, in tune with

orders: domination, control

orgy: free unrestricted sex, lust

orphan: alone, rejection

ostrich: clumsy, hiding your head in the sand, power bird

outside: unavailable, out of reach, abandoned

oven: waiting to be born, what's cooking? *See* Kitchens (page 122)

overdose: escapism, need for attention, plea for help, giving up

owl: wisdom, all-knowing, night bird

oyster: sensuality, sexual, treasure

p

packing: preparation, move, leaving behind the old

pain: set back, holding on too tightly, note where the pain is

palace: big plans, grand aspirations, reward

palm: honesty, truth, fate

paper: correspondence, statement, contract

parcel: surprise, the unknown, holding on too tightly

parents: authority figures, guardians, protectors

parrot: copy, one of the crowd, idle chatter

party: relaxation, fun, celebration

passport: new adventures, desire to get out

path: the way ahead, guidance, life's journey

peacock: finery, pride, make a show of yourself

pearl: wisdom, treasure

peas: copying, small irritations

pen: communication, commitment

pepper: spice up, who/what is getting up your nose?

perfume: aphrodisiac, sensual pleasure

photo: memory, remember, bring to mind

picnic: get out, relaxation, carefree

pigs: greed, laziness, pigs might fly

pillow: to cry into, softness, need for rest, magic potions

pin: irritation, pry into

plants: growth, new life

poetry: see things from a different viewpoint

pomegranates: sexual reproduction, new ideas

post: news, make effort

postman: bringer of news

potatoes: concern over lack, worry about the future

prayer: desperation, request for help
priest: authority figure, handing over power to
prison: feeling locked in, claustrophobic, guilt, shame
prostitute: degradation, servitude, sexual shame
pub: meeting place, social escapism
purse: holding tightly, fear of lack, female sexual organ

q

quarrel: expression of feelings, airing your views,
    confrontation, disagreement
queen: powerful female figure, in control, domineering
quiz: scrutinise, find solution to

r

rabbits: promiscuity, wildness, free spirit, magic. *See* Rabbits
    (page 99)
racehorse: power animal. *See* Horses (page 98)
rags: shedding of the old, loss of self esteem
railway: adventure, fresh possibilities, escape
rain: relief, letting go, cleansing, tears
rainbow: good omen, bright future
rake: go over issues, re-examine, scrutinise
ram: sexuality, male dominance. *See* Sheep and rams (page 101)
raven: messenger of news good and bad, be on alert
reading: relaxation, need for more information
relations: family gathering; what are their
    individual qualities?
reptiles: inner fears
rice: basic needs, wedding
riding: in control, skill, going for it, freedom
ring: commitment, completion, feeling trapped
road: life's journey, the way ahead
robbery: abused, violated, have you something others desire?
robin: good luck, new friend, sign of winter
rock: stability, foundations, stubbornness
rope: safety, bind, tie in, confinement, restriction
rose: love, passion, sensuality, beware of sharp thorns

rosemary: remembrance

rubbish: unwanted situations/relationships, clear out the old

run: escape, move away from, ambition, desire, determination, fear

rust: out of favour, no longer useful, outdated ideas/relationships

S

sack: surprise, the unknown good and bad

sage: purification, cleansing, ritual herb

sail: freedom, skills, riding the waves, positive omen. *See* Boats (page 76)

salad: nourishment, new life, freshness

salmon: riches, strength, power, determination

salt: preservation, cleansing, taste

sausages: phallic symbol

scabs: time to heal, friends you can't trust

school: conformity, regimentation, organisation, learning

science: need to understand, explanation, the mechanics of

scissors: sever, detachment, breaking away from

scream: call for help, distress. *See* Nightmares (page 41)

sea: mother/female figure, emotions, stability. *See* The sea (page 75)

sex: desire, your own sexuality, coming to terms with

shadow: your dark side, part of you, fear, unknown, being followed

shaving: exposing, cleansing, thoughtful decisions

shed: own space, need to be alone, rubbish store

sheep: following the crowd, lack of identity, a clone

ship: luxury, travel, holiday, adventure; note type of vessel. *See* Boats (page 76)

shipwreck: end of struggle, world falling apart. *See* Shipwreck (page 77)

shirt: formal occasion

shoes: progress, new venture

shops: choice, decision, money made available

shoulders: strength, support

shower: cleansing, refreshing, stimulating

sickness: health concerns, who/what is making you sick?

sight: vision, clarity, see forward

silk: luxury, sensuality

silver: values, promotion, commitment, engagement

singing: expressing views, rejoicing

sister: mirror image, rivalry

skin: protection, irritation

sky: far-reaching, no limits; if blue promising, if dark foreboding

sleep: need for rest, recuperation, time for self, time to dream

smoke: distraction, smoke screen, warning sign

soil: growth, new ideas waiting to be born, a cover-up

solider: discipline, routine, regimented, fighting for a cause

sores: life's bumps and bruises, intrusion, abuse, anger

sparrow: harmless, fickle

spider: spinning a web, waiting to pounce/strike, trapped

spin: confusion, take a risk

spit: disgust, anger

stag: male sexuality

star: hope, guidance, success

stardom: reward, achievement

sting: be on your alert, who is out to get you?

stomach ache: who/what can't you stomach? Digest thoughts

stranger: the unexpected, new opportunities, be open to new ideas

straw: reaping the rewards of hard work

strawberry: lusciousness, sensuality, naughty treats, good times ahead

sugar: false riches, disguise, pleasure

swan: beauty, unavailable

swear: oath, promise, need to express anger

sweet: temptation, lure, untrusting

sword: self-defence, stand up for yourself, protection, truth, honour

t

table: support, solidarity, function

talking: need to express yourself, clearing the atmosphere

tea: social ritual, idle chatter, time for a break. *See* Drinks (page 119)

tears: need to express yourself, emotional release, letting go

teeth: image, looks. *See* Teeth falling out (page 51)

telephone: communication, urgent contact, waiting to hear from someone

telescope: look closer, scrutinise

theatre: expression, pleasure, pretence

thighs: power, control, power over someone else, lust

thirst: nourishment, what/who do you thirst for?

throat: speech, need to express yourself, voice your thoughts

throne: ego, control, power over others

thunder: anger, take notice. *See* Thunder and lightning (page 91)

tiger: sexual desire, wildness. *See* Tigers (page 100)

time: pressure, take time out

toads: revulsion, the occult. *See* Frogs and toads (page 101)

toilet: need to let go of, dispose of, clear away rubbish, dump on

tomb: acknowledge the past, let go

tongue: speech, expression, taste, sensuality, taste

train: method of transport, get away, journey, life's journey. *See* Trains (page 127)

trap: setting a trap, being caught, scheming

treasure: reward, desire, greed

tree: stability, your body, family. *See* Trees (page 93)

tumours: fears, unexpressed pain/hurt, festering resentment

tunnel: temporary uncomfortable experience, new life ahead

turkey: take a chance, feeling stupid

u

ugly: revulsion, self-loathing, judgmental

umbrella: sheltering from emotions

underwear: feeling exposed, unprotected, alluring, sexual

v

valley: feeling down, pitfall

vegetables: energy, vitality, freshness, health; some vegetables have sexual implications

veil: secrets, hiding from something

velvet: luxury, warmth, richness, comfort

vicar: help, assistance, link with god

villa: escape, need to get away, holiday

vinegar: healing, cleansing, spite, vicious speech

violets: healing, sad loss, remembrance

violin: sorrow, tears, memories, accomplished skill, creative

virgin: innocence, challenge, inexperience

voice: expression, pay attention to

volcano: explosion, pouring out of emotions, destruction

vomit: unwanted feelings, rejection

vulture: greed, avarice, being picked on

w

walking: movement, moving forwards, making progress. *See* Walking (page 126)

walls: boundary, confinement, restrictions, frustration

war: fight, argument, expression of anger, fighting for what you want

washing: need to cleanse, purge, guilt, shame, feeling dirty

wasps: being got at, stung, under attack, venomous. *See* Biting and stinging insects (page 103)

watching: observation, take note of, bide your time

weapons: defence, protection, anger, lashing out, cowardice

web: trapped, no escape, need to break out, malicious gossip

wedding: celebration, commitment, new life

weeds: thwarted, choked, overwhelmed, pressurised

weighing: decisions, judging, comparing

well: emotional depths, deep fears, deep desires

wheat: nourishment, harvesting, rewards, security

wheel: on a treadmill, going round in circles, desire for progress

wheelbarrow: task needing hands-on hard work

whip: anger desiring vengeance, self-harm, sexual guilt, shame

whistling: contentment, happiness

widow: fear of abandonment, isolation, depression

windmill: slow steady progress

window: vision, see clearly, open opportunities

wine: celebration, importance of quality, decadence, opulence. *See* Alcohol (page 119)

witch: magic, you can make anything happen

wolves: intuition, wild urges, fear of your dark side

wood: solid, reliable, dependable

wool: warmth, comfort, security

workout: driven, determination, willpower, exercise

worm: get to the bottom of, reveal, work your way into

wounds: hurts, emotional pain, exposed feelings

writing: expression, accountability, commitment

y

yawn: bored, in need of rest

z

zebra: wild power animal, camouflage, hidden feelings

zoo: penned in, confusion, childhood pleasures

Afterword – Dream Thoughts

Perhaps we dream to communicate with the gods.

Perhaps our dream world is the gateway to other planets.

Perhaps dreaming is a key that releases us into other dimensions of time.

Do we meet in our dreams and exchange ideas with beings from other worlds?

Does the soul leave the body each time we dream?

Is dreaming the language of the gods?

If premonition dreams can show us the future ... then time cannot exist.

Is our dream world real and our waking life but a dream?

When we die do we wake up from life's dream?

Row, row, row the boat gently down the stream,

Merrily, merrily, merrily, merrily, life is but a dream!

AnnaStarsia

Index